Rescuing Curiosity
A WriteHive Anthology

Edited by
Justine Manzano

Rescuing Curiosity

Inked in Gray Press

InkedinGray.com

ISBN

Paperback: 978-1-952969-30-0

E-book: 978-1-952969-31-7

Cover Design by Maria Spada

CONTENTS

BEFORE YOU READ

LANGUAGE USAGE

Please note that some authors hail from outside the United States and have stories featuring UK English. Please don't be alarmed if you see some extra 'u's or an 's' where there would be a 'z' 😀

TRIGGER WARNINGS

Some stories contained within this anthology have trigger warnings. In full transparency, we will list them here if you need them. 🩶

"One Person's Nightmare," allusion to death of a parent and grandparents, allusion to emotional abuse; for "It Can't Be Sunday Everywhere at Once," allusion to global catastrophe

The Last Star: *reference child loss.*

The wisdom begins in wonder.
- Socrates

Foreword

In recent years, there's been a disturbing trend toward confirmation bias. We have witnessed an increase in book banning and a decrease of trust in science and subject matter experts. Instead of asking questions with genuine curiosity or researching with open minds, many have sought sources that simply affirm what they want to hear. Such echo chambers only lead to more echoes, compounding on distorted views and fears, and not an accumulation of truth and understanding.

What we need is a return to curiosity.

It is by asking questions and honestly seeking answers that we find paths toward better relationships and stronger, more hopeful futures. It is by embracing imagination and innovation that we enter new eras and grow as people. It is by being curious that we unravel more mysteries about our world and learn how to save it.

It's this concern about the loss of curiosity that inspired the name for this anthology, *Rescuing Curiosity*. Within these pages, you'll find a collection of stories that explore how asking questions, uncovering the past, or seeking new knowledge leads to a positive change in the lives and worlds of the characters.

And like the characters, I hope these pages inspire you to also learn and explore.

Be curious about the environment, about what affects it, harms it, and heals it. Be curious about those around you, about their wellbeing, their cultures, and their needs. Be curious about our past, about our failures, about our accomplishments, and how we can shape the future. Be curious about how we gained the rights we have now and what we stand to lose without them.

Especially be curious about what books are banned and why, what stories from history or marginalized communities others might keep to suppress. It is through this understanding of who we are, and how we came to be where we are today, that we can build the foundations for a brighter and more compassionate future.

Casting On

Emily Dodge

The tree is bare, the brown bark faded to gray. That's what life is now — barely varying shades of gray, the color stripped away years ago. I walk along the asphalt road until I come to my building. She stands outside by what used to be a maple, or maybe an oak. It's one of them, but without the fine dressing it's hard to tell. Her eyes rove over the tree, her hands jotting down notes.

"They're still the same," I say.

Linden slides the pen into the clipboard. "Is that what I should write down then?" She glances over to me, her eyes the color of slate, just like mine. Just like everyone else's. "The scientific opinion of the shop girl. I'm sure the institute will appreciate it." Her words are sharp as ever on this dull day. Sometimes it feels like they're the only thing that punctuates the monotony.

"Well, whatever you all are recording clearly isn't making a difference." I look at the tree, peering into the thin grooves of its bark as if there'll be some speck of color.

A small smirk catches on her face. "Not so sure if they're the same after all?"

I manage a small glare before I look away to find my key. My hand finds the cold metal and I hurry toward my building. "Well, enjoy watching bark," I call.

She huffs a laugh, pretending to turn back to the trees, but I can feel her eyes on me as I slip through the door. It's only when I'm inside that she returns to the careful note taking of how everything is exactly the same.

Even me.

After dinner, I settle into my chair and the fire lights up automatically. Even the flame flickers in shades of gray. I try to picture what it used to look like when I lit it by hand, but the memory is vague, hovering at the edges of my mind. I'm still trying to remember as I fall asleep.

The hours at the shop tick by the next day. The same customers come in, purchasing the same things. Sam, the delivery driver, arrives at one p.m. sharp, not a minute late. He unloads the truck, and I sort through everything. Then he drops one last box at my feet, the cardboard stained and peeling.

"What's this?" I nudge it with my foot.

He shrugs and tosses me the packing list. "It was in the truck." He leaves as I bend down and open the misshapen parcel.

A pair of sticks rest on top. No, not sticks. Knitting needles. There had still been color in the world the last time I knit. But the hobby had drifted away, sloughed out of my life as work became busy and time dwindled to stolen pieces of rest and not much more. Besides, they had made knitting needles that could knit by themselves, so what was the point? And then the color left, and I forgot all about them.

I pull the knitting needles out. There's more underneath, every possible size imaginable. The ends are a little dulled and the sides dinged, as if they've been used many times before. We can't sell them here. No one would want them, even if they were new. I pick up the box and move it to the side, planning to take it out to the dumpster when there's a chance.

The pale sun makes its way across the sky and customers keep coming and going. At ten to five, Harris comes in for their daily chocolate bar. The wrapper is gray, the bar inside too. They sigh as they place it on the counter. This is our normal exchange. I take their money and the sigh changes to a forced smile as they wait for their change. This time though, I don't just hand them the coins. This time I speak. Maybe it's the appearance of those knitting needles.

"Does it taste the same?" I ask.

Their eyes widen in surprise at my voice. "I like to think it does." Their hand hovers over the chocolate. "Well, maybe the memory of it at least."

"Is it enough?"

They pause like they've never considered that question before. But it's the one I've been considering all afternoon.

"I suppose it keeps this day moving." They pick up the bar and look down at it. "And that at least gives me the possibility of tomorrow." They smile at me as they leave. This time, it's not forced.

I lock up at closing, and I glance at the beaten down box with the knitting needles piled inside, next to other garbage. I hike it up, balancing it against my hip and head outside. The dumpster stands in the alley, the top tipped open, but I walk past, gripping the box a little tighter.

Linden is examining the trees again as I approach my building. Her body shifts slightly towards me like she's expecting my line. The same line I've said to her every day for years. But I can't — even if the tree looks exactly the same.

She looks at me, then back at the tree, her pen drumming incessantly against her clipboard. Finally, she clears his throat. " So what's in the box?"

"Oh, just some stuff we couldn't sell." I don't know why I don't say knitting needles.

"Well, the trees seem to be the same." She waits for my reply.

I nod as I head to my building. "Well, you would know."

"I would, but it's nice to hear a second opinion." Her mouth tugs into a small smile at the corner. It's something I haven't seen before. I would almost call it hopeful.

"Even from a shop girl?"

That cracks her smile wide open. "Especially from a shop girl."

My face flushes. I can feel it, even if I know it's just an ashen pallor. I glance over to the tree. "Well then. I suppose it's still the same."

She jots something down with her pen. "Noted."

There's a flutter in my stomach, the tiniest beating of something that hasn't been there in ages. But I just grip the box tighter and nod, fighting back a smile as I head inside.

That night, I sit in the same overstuffed chair after dinner. The fire flickers, the light catching all the shades of gray.

Until it doesn't.

My eyes snap open and I scramble toward the box, my hands digging through the knitting needles. And then I find it. It's green — honest to goodness green. Not a rich green, but light, like the trembling colors that first emerge in spring. Or what I remember of spring. My hands reach for it, pausing like it will disappear the moment I touch it. But then it's in my fingers, the soft fibers running over my hand. It's yarn.

I pick up the nearest needles and hold the yarn up to them, waiting for the automatic clack. But there's nothing. No magic, no automation. If I want something crafted from that color, I'll have to do it. My hands shake trying to remember the steps. They keep shaking, but I manage to cast on a single, wobbly stitch. The yarn is so green against that gray, I forget I haven't done this for years. So I cast another, and another.

A pile of knitted, slightly crooked things sits in my lap by the time I'm done. The light outside the window has paled to a gentle silver from the leaden night. The sun isn't far away. I scoop everything into my arms and head outside. I don't even think as I stop underneath the tree by my building.

It takes until the colourless dawn for me to finish, my hands aching with the effort. But the pain is sweet, the memory of how much they've done over the last several hours. There's a hundred, maybe two hundred. Two hundred knitted spring-green leaves fluttering on the tree. They're far from perfect. Most are lopsided, a little lumpy. It's not the magic that used to make the needles knit by themselves, but it feels like another kind. A better kind.

I can't wait for Linden to see them, to see the difference in this day, but she won't be here for hours, so I force myself to go to work. I down cup after cup of nearly flavorless coffee, the machine brewing it on a continuous loop. I know the liquid is gray, but my mind still rings with the color green. Sam drops off the day's deliveries. There are no extra boxes, but that's okay. Color has already come back. It'd be selfish to ask for more, and I don't need it. Harris comes in for their chocolate. They smile before they even grab the bar.

"It's the strangest thing," they start.

Did they see it? Did they see the leaves? I wonder how many have seen them by now, how much that color sparks this *something* in others, the way it has for me.

"It almost tasted different last night." They hold the chocolate in their hand as if it'll change into something more. "Silly, isn't it?" They smile once more, one almost tinged with sadness. I reach over the counter and place my hand on theirs.

"It's not silly," I say. "Maybe it was different. Maybe this one will be too."

It will all be different now, I'm certain. Harris smiles again. This time it's wide and beautiful, and the grayness in them lifts away for a brief moment. It's the leaves, even if they haven't seen them.

"Well, I'll let you know . . . if it's different." They wave goodbye and leave, but more people come in. The customers seem brighter as the day goes on. There's no color in their skin, or hair, or eyes, but the gray is different somehow. The end of the day finally comes, and I lock the shop and hurry out.

She'll be there by the trees, and this time something will finally be different. I race around the corner, and my heart constricts in my chest. Linden's not there. And neither are the leaves. The tree is bare, back to the same monotonous pallor it's been for years. Every trace of that spring-green is gone.

Every piece of hope I had stitched into myself unravels. This can't have happened. I run into my building and find the box, my chest constricting, like iron bars caving in on my lungs and heart. Crushing them into ruin. I dig through the box, throwing the needles aside, but there's no more yarn, not even a scrap. There's no more chance for color in this world.

The next day dawns gray, and the horror of it finally hits me. Maybe I was already numb all those years ago when the color first left, but I remember now, and the pain rips through in a fresh and terrible way. Work drags by and it's the same. When Sam brings the deliveries, there are no extras.

The customers seem as heavy as they have always been, though I never really noticed until now. Harris pauses as they pay for their chocolate bar, like they want to smile, to say something, but the look on my face must stop them because they drop the coins on the counter and hurry out. I barely notice when the clock signals it's closing time.

She's there this time, by the bare tree, clipboard in hand as if yesterday never happened, as if there hadn't been a bright burst of color rippling by our spot. I want to scream, to tear that damn tree apart piece by piece, shredding the bark until it's a gray pile of *nothing*. Because that's what this life is now. What it has been. I just never realized it.

I hurry past her so she doesn't have time to say anything. I can't bear the same lines. Not now. I spend the evening, as always, by the soot-colored fire until my eyelids are so heavy, there's no point in keeping them open.

The next day, Sam brings the deliveries at exactly one p.m.. There are no spare boxes again, but I already knew there wouldn't be. He puts the last box down and I sign the slip. He turns and heads back toward his truck. It's barely noticeable, but it's there. A piece of the green yarn, tied around his hair. I'm so shocked, I can't even say anything before he drives away. But that speck stays with me. In the afternoon, Harris comes in and picks up their chocolate. They don't say anything as they hand me the coins, but I see it all the same. A small scrap of green around their wrist.

"It's definitely different," they say. "Better than the memory." Harris gives me a knowing look and leaves. With each new customer, I search for a piece of that green. And many carry it — even if it's only the smallest of strings.

She's there, again, but this time there's no clipboard. Instead she holds a strand of green. It rests softly on her fingers, like she's scared that it will disappear if she grips too hard, like it will unravel.

Her eyes meet mine as I make it to the tree. She holds out the fiber and we each take an end, the green strung between us.

"You have to say it," she says. "For official records." She doesn't try to fight the smile on her face and motions to the tree.

And there it is. Not a piece of green yarn. It's barely even a color. But it's there. A deep reddish brown on a small patch of bark. It's coming back.

No — it *is* back.

"It's not the same," I finally say.

"No, it's not."

I laugh and lift the piece of yarn, her hand following mine. The wind catches it and carries it off, but this time there's no pain in my heart at the loss.

There will be more yarn, and the world will be a riot of color.

ABOUT EMILY DODGE

Emily Dodge is a prize winning author who lives in Nova Scotia with her family. When not writing, or working as an environmental educator, she can be found outdoors, unless it's impossibly rainy, and then she can be found reading or attempting to knit something, poorly.

One Person's Nightmare

Dawn Vogel

When I was young, I had a nightmare that wouldn't go away. I would wake up in my dad's old bedroom in my grandma's converted attic and see a dragon, black as night with glowing red eyes like fire inside a blackened log creeping up the stairs toward me. The sound of an old-time radio atop the dresser, with a man's voice speaking, played in the background.

And always, *always*, I woke up terrified.

Never once did the dragon make it past the top of the stairs. Never once was I harmed in any way. But I knew, if I hadn't been able to wake up, the dragon would have slithered across the dark linoleum attic floor and gobbled me up. Somehow, the voice droning on the radio made the whole thing worse, even though I couldn't remember what the man said.

I'm not sure whether I was more afraid of the dragon or the voice. Logically, it made sense that it was the dragon. But when I thought back, it might have been the voice.

The nightmare stopped recurring, eventually. As I got older, we didn't stay over at my grandma's house as often, or at all. I went back once, as an adult, before she died, but I didn't go upstairs.

She was gone now, and so was my dad. But the house was still there. There was a tiny part of me that always wanted to go back, even though it had been years since anyone in my family lived there. But how would you address the new residents, who might not have been the ones who bought it from her, or whichever cousin was the executor of her estate?

You waited until it went back on the market.

It felt weird to drive myself there and park the car. To not be in my parents' van, none of my siblings clambering out. The air lacked that wintertime bite it almost always had when we visited. The neighborhood looked different when it wasn't lit up with Christmas lights, when there wasn't ice on the small front lawn to crunch across, even though the sidewalk was shoveled clear.

It was close enough to sunset, though, that the attic light was on, and the small window in the room that had been my dad's cast a golden square of light onto the front walkway.

I skirted that light as I walked up for the open house.

The realtor met me at the door, all smiles and handshakes. She launched into her sales pitch, but I tuned it out as I took in the living room. The house didn't smell like it always had, and the décor was all new. Tasteful, of course, but it felt wrong. It was too sterile, with no photos of grandchildren or tchotchkes from all over the world.

A couple came in behind me, and the realtor turned her attention to them, with a quick "let me know if you have any questions" directed at me.

The door to the attic hung open, like a waiting maw, light spilling into the ground-floor hallway beyond the dining room. The stairs had been redone, probably to remove the asbestos-laden linoleum of the 1940s. Now they were honey-colored wood or, more likely, laminate, bright and inviting. But they were still the same stairs to me, still the path the dragon took to the attic.

I climbed the stairs slowly, holding the railing like I did as a child. White curtains hung over the window at the top of the stairs, overlooking the postage-stamp backyard that only the dogs ever seemed to use when my grandparents lived here.

The former play space that took up the bulk of the attic had been transformed into a mini library, with half-height book-cases lining one side, butted up against the knee wall beneath the steeply pitched ceiling. The light was brighter than it had been during my childhood, the space softened with a large beige area rug, fluffy and plush beneath my feet. A pair of low-slung chairs occupied the space under the other slope of ceiling and roof.

And in the back, the door, which had never been closed when I was younger, separated my dad's old room from the rest of the space. Even if I hadn't been accustomed to it being open, it seemed odd to close it during an open house. The listing claimed three bedrooms, and though I hadn't looked at any of them, I knew there were two on the first floor, flanking the single bathroom, leaving this upstairs space the only possible place for a third bedroom.

I didn't want to snoop, but I couldn't help but be curious. I approached the door, fumbling for a doorknob that wasn't there. What I had expected to be the door was a featureless, flat piece of wood, the same warm honey color as the two closet doors to either side. I opened each of those in turn, thinking maybe someone had remodeled the space with a different entrance. But the closets were still there, dusty and scented with mothballs.

I pressed on the wood covering the entrance to my dad's old room, then tried to slide it, then knocked gently. It didn't budge. I was certain I had seen light coming from the window I knew was on the other side, though. Why would someone light an unused space?

In the small library, behind the chairs, was more of the honey-colored plywood, all stained to match throughout this floor. When we were kids, that area behind the knee walls had been storage for toys, kept tucked away when we weren't visiting, covered by those plywood panels that could be moved aside on track-mounted rollers.

We'd always been leery of that space, which was unlit and unfinished. But we'd peeked in there now and then. I knew it ran the length of the house.

And I knew my dad's old room had similar access panels to this main room.

I listened at the top of the stairs, hand on the faux wrought-iron railing framing the stairwell on two sides. Multiple voices filtered up — it seemed the realtor had her hands full.

I slid one of the access panels to the side. The space beyond held the same dry, dusty smell I remembered, but none of the toys or boxes of holiday decorations that had been there before. Tucking my cellphone between my bra strap and chest, with the built-in flashlight shining forward into the space, I crawled in, scooting across the rough boards toward my dad's old room, careful not to bump up against the exposed insulation in the rafters.

Reaching the portion of the space adjoining my dad's old room, I scrabbled at the nearest access panel until I found the edge of a board and could slide it along the track. It moved sluggishly, rubbing up against the comforter on the twin bed that had been snugged up against the wall, just like it had been when I was younger.

The bed moved easily enough once I got my hands on it, sliding across the floor without a sound, and I clambered out. The light here was on, as I'd seen from the walkway, casting that golden glow across the room that had not changed since I was a child.

As I took it in, though, I realized the room *had* changed. Where the walls had been plain and white, drawings now covered every inch. They weren't new, though. The lowest drawings were those of a child, but as they ascended the walls, they improved in quality, like an artist learning more and more about their craft.

They were drawings of fantastical animals — unicorns and griffins, scandalously topless mermaids and centaurs — surrounded by castles, forests, lakes, and more.

And there, just above the space where the bed I'd moved normally sat, the dragon from my dreams.

I choked back a gasp of surprise. The dragon was rendered in a careful hand — the sinuous body, the gleaming scales, the glowing red eyes, even the smoke rising from its nostrils. My dad, years before I was born, as a young boy or teenager, had drawn the dragon that haunted my nightmares.

I couldn't have known about these drawings as a child. They'd been covered with paint then, hidden from view. Knowing my grandmother, she'd had my grandfather do it as soon as my dad moved out at eighteen. Only now, somehow, they'd bled through the paint. The realtor had probably closed off this room until she had time to have it repainted.

I reached out, tentative, and brushed my hand across the drawing of the dragon.

I hadn't expected it to writhe under my touch, nor had I anticipated the radio, an antique even when I was a child, to click on.

For the first time in my life, the voice on the radio spoke words I could understand. "You have returned."

I took a step back. "Wha?"

"Hmmm, no. Not him. Part of him. Ah. You are the girl child. The eldest."

I pressed my hands to my ears to block out the sound of my oldest nightmare, quivering and shying away from the radio. "This can't be happening."

Though it should have been muffled, the voice remained clear. "You are the one I tried to talk to all those years ago."

My jaw dropped, and I pulled my hands from my ears. "What . . . who are you?"

"He called me Mynaessairth the Devourer, but that is a complicated name. You may call me Myn."

"Myn." I pointed at the drawing. "You're . . . my dad drew you."

"Yes."

"And when I was a kid, you were in my nightmares."

A long sigh came from the radio. "They were not meant to be nightmares. But I was locked away, and my voice could not reach you."

"Right. And now?"

"Now, perhaps, you have reached the point in your life where his struggles make sense to you, and thus my voice becomes clear."

Struggles? I knew my dad had clashed with his parents, but what teenager hadn't? Was there more I didn't know? "What struggles?"

"His parents were focused on reality, but he dreamed of a world beyond the one you call home. He drew me and the others into existence, naming each of us and giving us stories, dreaming of the day when he would leave home and search for us. In return, we helped him find his freedom."

"Freedom?" I arched an eyebrow. "He joined the military."

"It was freedom for him to be out from under this roof."

I sat on the bed, hard. Tension had always simmered between our dad and grandma. In his final years, he'd had no kind words for his mother. But to me, she was our fun grandma, who took us on adventures our parents didn't, giving each of her grandchildren time to spend away from their siblings and be the sole object of her attention.

Here in this space, having seen the artwork and heard Myn's explanation, I started to put the pieces together in a different way. She'd probably discouraged my dad's art, hence why he'd stopped creating and never talked about it.

But its presence in this space where I spent long hours as a child had seeped into my subconscious and resurfaced as my recurring nightmare. Myn and the others helped my dad find his freedom. But once my dad had left, what else was Myn to do but protect the artwork from those who would have erased it?

If I'd been able to understand Myn's voice on the radio as a child, maybe I would have understood and helped my dad keep his secrets. But knowing the sort of kid I was, I would have run to tell my grandma, and she'd have made my grandpa, or maybe even my dad, tear out the old plaster and replace it to destroy every trace of the old artwork. Now, with none of them alive to do anything about it, was it safe for me to understand the story?

I couldn't stay here much longer, lest the realtor get suspicious at my absence or worse, overhear this conversation. "Myn, I have to go, and I won't be back. As much as I love this house, it's more space than I need, and I'm not in the market to move. Is there anything else . . . is there anything I can do for you?"

"You have the ability to carry our stories out of this place, a freedom he never had."

"How?" I asked.

"Record the drawings he made, and listen for me in your dreams again. I will tell you our stories. You can decide what you want to do with them then."

I nodded, pulling my phone out from where it was still tucked in my shirt, still shining the beam of the flashlight around the small room, despite the overhead light. I took a picture of the radio and a few stills of the drawings, then stood in the center of the room and rotated, recording every bit of artwork.

"Thank you, Myn," I said quietly.

In response, the radio clicked off.

I maneuvered myself back into the space under the rafters, pulling the bed back into place and closing the access panel.

The realtor and the couple she'd been showing the upstairs space blinked when I crawled out into the small library.

"Sorry, I just needed to get a sense of the storage space up here," I said, brushing dust and cobwebs out of my hair. "It's got quite a bit, but it probably needs a Roomba or something to tidy it up."

"Good to know," the realtor replied, her voice tight and smile stiff.

She didn't ask how I knew to look for the storage space, which hadn't been pictured in the listing. I suppose it was weird enough seeing me creep out of there, flashlight beam shining from the center of my upper chest. But she must have known about the artwork, which was why the room had been closed off in the first place.

"Anyway, thanks for the open house, and good luck!" I said, scooting past the potential buyers, down the stairs, and out into the night.

When I got back into my car, I let myself cry as I looked through the photos on my phone, which had captured my dad's artwork with stunning precision. I traced their lines on the screen, remembering the electronic schematics he used to draw, and seeing where some of those lines picked out the same fantastical shapes as his younger drawings had.

Soon enough, I'd learn their names and their stories, thanks to Myn's promise. Maybe I'd write them down, to share with the rest of the family. Or maybe I'd finally understand my dad all the better and keep them to myself. Either way, it was closure — for my dad's dreams, and for my nightmares.

ABOUT DAWN VOGEL

Dawn Vogel has written for children, teens, and adults, spanning genres, places, and time periods. More than 100 of her stories and poems have been published by small and large presses. Her specialties include young protagonists, siblings who bicker but love each other in the end, and things in the water that want you dead. She is a member of SFWA and Codex Writers. She lives in Seattle with her awesome husband (and fellow author), Jeremy Zimmerman, and their cats. Visit her at historythatneverwas.com or on BlueSky @historyneverwas.

Lila & Snake

Laura L. Dennis

It had been seven days since Lila had seen the snake, and she still had not told anyone. She had her reasons. For one, the villagers had enough on their minds with the stream. It no longer filled up the way it used to, not even after a good rain, but rather glided along several inches below its banks, diminishing at times to a mere trickle and once, to an oozy mud. The village did its best to take the changes in stride; so far, thankfully, the cisterns had not gone below half-full.

Another problem was that Lila could not be sure it even was a snake. True, the instant the creature fell on her, the word *snake* had popped into her mind, accompanied by a cold undercurrent she recognized as fear, although the reaction did not feel like her own. She tried to remember the description once shared by a visitor — at once sinuous and scaly, with eyes that didn't close and a flickering tongue — but it did not help all that much. No snakes had been seen in this area since the last big floods more than a century before.

Lila's biggest problem, however, was that she had been

asleep when it happened. She kept trying to catch her mother alone to ask what she thought, but with her father away from home, her mother had her hands full with Council duties and Lila's older brother Jacob. Jacob was a lout of a boy as omnipresent and exasperating as a second shadow. No way would she talk about this in front of him. He no longer teased her about her dreams the way he used to, but that was mainly because the damage was already done. Although the other kids mostly left her alone now that she had learned to keep her mouth shut, she had heard the whispers. Soon she would be old enough to start going out on Expeditions, but no one wanted her in their group.

Lila felt equal parts excited and afraid when she thought about this change to her role in the life of the village. Settled by people seeking refuge from floods, famine, and other disasters near and far, the village had set up its system of rotating roles before her great-great-grandmother was born. Older children cared for the younger ones, tended the gardens, and worked in the orchards, while adults took turns serving on the Council, caring for those in need, and going out on Expeditions. These left every full moon, in groups of four to eight, men and women combined, and returned sometime between the quarter and crescent moon to tell of any changes in the land and to share the medicine and food they had foraged. Children joined these Expeditions as apprentices once they turned sixteen.

Additionally, groups of five villagers were sometimes chosen for special Learning Expeditions that spent anywhere from three to six moons in a much larger settlement, a place the elders said was once called Pittsburgh. There, they traded news with other travelers, bought supplies the villagers could not produce themselves, and visited buildings that housed books, recordings, and films. Most such items had been lost when the sea crashed over the coasts of what some people called America, others Turtle Island. The only way to consult what remained of these precious stores of knowledge was to travel to the places that protected them. In Lila's village, everyone made this journey at least once. Some hated the time away from home and complained of getting lost in the mazes of buildings and crowds. Lila's parents Adeline and Rohan, however, were among those who moved easily between the two worlds; this explained Rohan's absence for the past two moons.

LILA WAS CURRENTLY ASSIGNED to work in the berry patch. As she picked strawberries one afternoon, being careful only to pick those that were perfectly ripe, Lila wondered what kind of traveler she would be. She admired her parents, yet sometimes felt their adventurous spirits ran a bit too high, a trait magnified in her brother who, as a second-year apprentice, constantly pushed the limits of what his Expedition leaders would allow. Until recently, she would have been content to stay in the refuge of her dreams, but these no longer felt quite as safe. Had the creature in her dream been a snake? If so, why hadn't that long-ago visitor mentioned that snakes could talk? She hoped her father would come home soon so she could get uninterrupted time with her mother, and also so she could ask her father what he thought about what she had seen.

As she moved down the row, the dream looped once more through her mind. She had been walking the path that circled the village when the animal fell out of a tree, landed on her shoulder, and promptly slithered into a corner, the forest having morphed into a room in the way her dreamscapes so often did.

A damp leaf brushed against her leg, startling her back to the present. The way she jumped reminded her of the fearful undercurrent she had felt in the dream, though she sensed that her emotion had been nothing compared with that of the trembling creature.

"Hi there," she had said. "I'm Lila. Please don't be afraid. I'm nice, I promise."

"I know," he had replied.

Before Lila could ask what exactly it was he knew, her stupid brother had awakened her by yanking the rope that secured her hammock, sending her tumbling to the ground.

THE CREATURE RETURNED in the middle of strawberry season, one night when she was deep in sleep, almost as if she had conjured him. This time, he wound himself loosely like a limp rope, showing not a single sign of agitation.

"Hello," he said.

"Hello," replied Lila. "Who are you?"

"I have many names."

"Tell me one. Please," she added as he changed positions, looking like he might flee.

"I was there at the beginning," he said enigmatically.

Lila had no idea what he meant by that. She changed tack.

"Can I call you Snake?"

"If you would like."

With that, he wriggled through a crack in the wall. He came back a few nights later, and again the next three nights, staying longer every time. The fifth night, however, he stayed away. The next day, Lila made more than her usual share of mistakes, pulling up strawberry plants instead of weeds. Elena, the girl in charge of that day's harvest, trudged off to tell Adeline she thought Lila might be unwell.

Mother and daughter walked back to their dwelling in

silence. As they entered, Adeline asked, "Is everything okay, mon trésor?"

Lila smiled at the endearment. She opened her mouth to confide just as Jacob bounded into the room, filling the space with his bulky frame. How could he be just two years older yet more than twice her size?

"Yeah," she muttered. "I'm fine."

She felt her mother's eyes on her as she turned away, but now was not the time to explain. She could never predict when Snake would show up, nor what he would do or say when he did. Sometimes he zigzagged across the dreamscape telling funny stories, while other times he lay flat and dejected along the wall. Several times he told her the village needed to watch the water, which puzzled Lila. That was all the Council did these days. Asking him to elaborate, however, proved pointless, as he always answered with some sort of riddle or goofy joke.

"Do you know why you can't trust me?"

"No."

"Because I speak with a forked tongue."

She fell for this a few times before she caught on. The first time she blurted out the answer, he dove into a hole in the floor without a sound. She wondered if she had offended him by not playing along.

THE FOLLOWING MORNING, Lila woke to panicked shouts from over by the stream. She pulled on pants and a shirt from a pile of shared clothes and went to see what the yelling was about.

Water rushed down, raucous and muddy, more than anyone in the village had ever seen. While showers had fallen for several days, no amount of rain had filled the creek bed with water for some time now. The dwellings were set high enough above the stream to be protected, and the tough-rooted mix of grass and sedge, planted when Lila's grandmother was small, retained the soil, but still, the sudden wild flow troubled them.

Lila realized she could not keep worrying about Jacob. She had to tell her mother about Snake. Adeline listened carefully, asked some questions, then to Lila's surprise, invited her to the Central Fire, where the Council would convene that very night.

ADULTS SERVED on the Council for six moons at a time. During that time, they filled in around the village wherever they were needed but did not participate in any Expeditions until their time as councilor was done. Any councilor could call a meeting; given the events of that morning, no one argued when Adeline did just that.

Several members of the circle seemed to think the creek's strange behaviors were caused by something they called a dam. Lila had no idea what that could be. Judging by the somber expressions on the councilors' faces, though, it was serious. It was agreed that at the next full moon, an Expedition would head upstream as far as they could go in search of an answer. The Council would reconvene upon their return.

"Before we adjourn," Adeline said, "I'd like us to hear from Lila."

Lila gulped and stared down at the faint brown hairs that speckled her calves and toes.

"We all know that Lila sometimes has dreams," Adeline continued.

Lila looked up, glad for the shadows that concealed the flush of heat creeping onto her face. She had not mentioned the dreams to anyone besides her mother for so long. People still talked about them? Embarrassed, she returned her gaze to her feet, peering up through teary lashes at the circle of councilors, sure she would see traces of her brother's mockery. The councilors, however, remained as solemn as they had been when discussing the dam.

"I think you should hear from her," her mother concluded. "Lila? Look up, mon cœur."

With a shuddering breath, Lila told the assembly about the creature, about his jokes and his sadness, and above all, about his warning.

"The thing is," she said, "I'm not even sure snake is the right word. It's not like I've ever seen one."

"Describe it," said Maeve, an older woman with sandy hair and aqua eyes that reminded Lila of the nearby fishing hole.

"Him. No disrespect intended," Lila added quickly. "It's just he talks like we do, so he feels like a him. But at the same time, he moves so differently. He doesn't have legs or arms or hands or feet. He can climb trees and he can make the funniest shapes. Sometimes he curls himself up real small and plays hide-and-seek in my dreamspace."

"Does he frighten you?" asked Maeve.

Lila considered. "Not me, no. But sometimes I get this feeling when he shows up, like there's another person somewhere deep inside me who might be afraid."

"That could be an ancestor," Maeve said thoughtfully. "My grandmother's grandmother used to tell of a man who drove all the snakes off their island."

"I can see why," said her sister Mary. "I mean, a snake tricked the first people into leaving Paradise."

"Hold on a minute. Not everyone believes that's what happened," interrupted Paul as he ran his dark-skinned fingers through the tight gray twists of his hair.

"Lots of people do though," Mary and Maeve said, almost in unison.

Aditi, the newest member of the Council, said thoughtfully,

"I remember an old story my paranani used to tell of how her ancestors kept shrines to snakes to protect their land in Kerala."

Kayashuta's long black hair shone in the firelight. "Akso:dgo:wa:h always said Serpent could mean many things. In some stories, such creatures signify anger and destruction. In others, they bring fertility and the promise of a fresh start. Have you asked him which one he is?"

"He's not much for answering. He lets me call him Snake, he says he has been there since the beginning, and he seemed to know what would happen this morning. That's pretty much it," Lila answered.

The talk continued as each councilor shared the different snake legends they had heard. Lila could connect some of the names and stories with the creature in her dream, but not all. The initial rush of pleasure at being taken seriously gave way to confusion. She almost wished her dreams were still just jokes to the other children, that she could bury her head in her mother's lap. Just as she was going to ask to be excused, however, the conversation steered back to her.

"Lila? What do you think?"

Lila blinked, unsure. "I don't think any of these stories are Snake." She shook her head in frustration, the way she did when a bug got caught in her half-combed curls. "What I mean is all of these stories could be Snake." She stopped again. "No, not that either. I think it's closest to what Kayashuta said. I feel like Snake holds a lot of stories. But I don't know. I thought I was just here because of what he said about the water."

The circle watched her, clearly hoping for more, but Lila had nothing left. Finally, Kayashuta stepped in. "You did well to tell us, Lila. Snake clearly trusts you. Keep listening."

"Yes," said Anastasios. "And tell us everything."

"No," said Adeline, sharply. "We don't know yet if everything Snake says has meaning. I trust Lila will know what stories to share and when to share them."

Lila's heart puddled in gratitude as she silently beseeched the others to agree. Decisions only counted if they were unanimous.

"I concur," said Aditi.

"So do I," added Kayashuta, followed by Paul.

The others joined in, some more reluctantly than others, as Adeline fastened her violet eyes on each of them in turn, deploying her uncanny ability to make others seek her approval. Lila wondered briefly if her mother's influence was the only reason they all agreed, then realized she did not care. She and Snake were safe.

The thought startled her.

Why had she thought they were in danger?

THE NEXT EXPEDITION stayed out longer than usual, eventually discovering two settlements beyond their usual range. In the first, the inhabitants described episodes similar to those Lila's village had experienced, stories of a gentle, largely predictable stream grown capricious, with no apparent explanation for the change. Two of their residents joined the party, which two days later discovered a dam erected by the inhabitants of a third village farther upstream. In the recent rains, the resulting body of water had overflowed its designated area and so the villagers had removed part of the barrier to release the surplus in one great gush. The representatives of the downstream villages explained the frightening and potentially destructive effects this practice could have. The dam-builders listened, placid smiles on their faces, as they all shared a meal of grilled fish and foraged fruits and greens. They said they saw the threat the sudden release of excess water could pose. Assuming this meant the dam would be removed or at least modified, the Council declared the Expedition a success.

ANOTHER MOON PASSED and with it, any sign of rain. Large patches of dry sand emerged where the stream had been. By the time the Learning Expedition returned, the village had resorted to rationing water.

Despite a steady rainfall in the week following their return, the situation remained precarious. Rohan and the others had barely gotten used to sleeping in their own hammocks when the Council voted to send them back to the city in search of solutions to the predicament in which the village found itself. Lila's father promised that while there, he would see if he could find other instances of people who had experiences similar to hers with Snake, who had not only returned, but also had now taken up residence in her dreamscape night and day. She rarely knew what he would do next, nor did she always see how the world in her head connected to the one outside. Sometimes, he spelled it out for her right away, as when he pestered her to walk to a tree just beyond the village on an afternoon she would have preferred to nap instead. When she — they — arrived, she discovered an expanse of truffles and was praised for the promise she showed as a soon-to-be apprentice forager.

Other times, it took a while before she understood what meaning Snake's words and actions held. When Elena's abuelito died, for example, Lila remembered how Snake had once told her of an indigo world full of twinkling light and swirling golden souls. Despite feeling shy, she shared the vision with the grieving girl.

"Do you think my grandfather is there?" Elena asked.

"I do," Lila answered, realizing that what she said felt right.

"Tell me more."

Lila obliged, talking late into the night as she moved from

visions to epic tales. By the time the sun rose, she had her first real friend, one whose tears had dried, despite or perhaps because of Snake's awful jokes.

"Why can't you throw snakes like boomerangs?

"Because they'll come back to bite you."

Lila tried to tell Snake that she didn't like this one — everyone knew she would never hurt him, and besides, she had never seen him even think about biting anyone. Not to mention the small problem of him existing only in her head. Far from being persuaded by this argument, he kept on.

"Why do you have to measure snakes in inches?

"Because they don't have any feet."

Along with the girls' budding friendship, a new ritual emerged. When a crop was harvested or an Expedition returned, the older villagers feasted and danced, and the younger children played. The village's energy spent, their attention would turn to Lila, who would share a few of Snake's many tales. Even Jacob and his friends found themselves enthralled by the stories of Anahuac, a far-off place where Snake's kind had been adorned in feathers centuries before. Elena, for her part, took to referring to Snake as Quetzal, short for Quetzalcoatl, though the nickname never really caught on.

MEANWHILE, the stream remained unpredictable, subject less to seasons and weather than to the will of a people whom the villagers increasingly suspected of having ungenerous spirits, despite the shared meals and even-tempered smiles. Jacob and his cronies, who had just completed their apprenticeships and were now eligible to be full-fledged Expedition members, formed a team of their own to take back the stream, ready to use force if need be. Knowing the Council would not approve, they slipped out in the dead of night. Unfortunately for them, Snake warned Lila, who told her parents. Rohan and Adeline brought the group back within the hour.

"What do you think about all this?" Lila asked Snake one night, shortly before she was supposed to leave on her first-ever foraging Expedition. "And don't go acting all silly or mysterious. I'm serious."

"I think they must feel very afraid," Snake replied.

"Who? My brother and his band of idiots?"

Snake, apparently unable to help himself, replied indirectly. "The memory of thirst is long and frightening."

Lila pondered this. "Maybe. But right now, only the upstream village has a way out of that. How many Expeditions have we sent? The middle village doesn't even bother to send anyone anymore. No matter how many times we explain what's happening down here, those people keep acting the exact same way."

"True," said Snake. "But so do all of you."

Discomfort roiled in Lila's belly. In the morning, she told her parents what Snake had said.

Adeline summoned the Council.

Lila walked carefully, keeping an even distance between two more experienced members of the Expedition, which was heading upstream once again; this time, Lila and Snake were to help negotiate. Her nerves were settled by the weight of her supply basket on her back; it forced her to pay attention and kept her feet firmly connected to the ground. When the Council had decided that this, rather than foraging, should be her first mission, she had assumed Snake would give her plenty of ideas on what to say. Instead, he had been absent for several days now, filling her with a growing sense of dread.

As the party broke camp on their last day of outbound travel, she spotted what she took at first to be a length of dull green twine coiled on top of her pack. Then she understood.

"Why hello, Snake!" she cried. "I'm so glad you're here!"

"How are you feeling?" he asked.

It took her a minute to understand that even though she could see him, his voice still existed only in her head.

"Better now that you're here. But how come you're not talking? For real, I mean. Out loud."

"Not everyone will be happy to see me, Lila. There are those who have their reasons for distrusting a talking snake. Others will see me as an intruder even if I don't talk, and you and me together, well, that could complicate things. If we want them to listen, we need to proceed with caution. Especially me."

"But . . ."

"I don't have a butt." Snake laughed at his pun.

"Very funny."

"I know. Now make room for me in this basket."

Lila rolled her eyes as she removed some tools from a smaller basket within her pack. Snake curled into it with a look Lila could have sworn was a wink, though she had long since learned snakes had no eyelids. She tucked the smaller basket back into place, shoved the scattered smaller articles around it, shouldered her load, and fell into line.

Lila spotted the dam from some distance away. It was built just past where two streams converged, creating a body of water much larger than their own naturally formed fishing hole. Although she had come here expecting to hate it, she had to admit there was something in the large, still pool that calmed and attracted her. Equally surprising was the fact that the residents were not at all hostile. Other Expeditions had said as much, of course; she realized now she had not truly believed them. She began to understand what Snake had meant. Neither group wished to fight. Still — how would they ever find a way out of this?

The Expedition's camp was scarcely distinguishable from the village, whose inhabitants had spent more time building the dam and a fleet of rafts and canoes than houses and other structures. Intrigued despite herself, Lila looked at the vessels for so long that a woman called Hali offered to take her for a ride. The sensation atop the raft was strange, almost weightless, with a tinge of peril that sent a thrill down Lila's spine. She even dared to trail her hand in the water. They returned to a meal of grilled fish, the same meal this village served all visitors, to which her team added their foraged goods, this time consisting of mushrooms and berries.

Her earlier thrill gone, Lila found herself torn between savoring the flaky meat and worrying over what was to come.

Snake sensed her concern. "Stop it," he said. "Don't you trust me?"

"No, I do." Lila tried to sound convincing.

"Then do what I say. Get me out of your pack — no, keep me in the basket — and go get one of the spare canteens. Singing builds up quite a thirst."

"Wait, what?"

"You're going to sing the story while I rise up out of this basket and dance."

Lila stifled a giggle. "You? Dance?"

"Yes," he said curtly. "Me. They are going to think you are charming me with your song. They won't know that it's the other way around."

"Sorry. My father told me it was another kind of snake that did that," Lila replied.

"Maybe it is. But I don't see why they should have all the fun. Besides, it's part of the plan."

"Plan?" Lila fretted. "What plan? What if I get it wrong? I haven't even been to the city yet. I don't know how to do this."

"Yes, you do. You don't need the city. You and I, we have our own kind of knowledge."

Lila mulled this over as Snake went on. "We will hear music no one else does. You will sing the song while I bend and twist in time. Together, we will create a kind of spell, the kind that tells a story."

"What sort of story?"

"Stories where everyone has enough."

"Stories?" Lila emphasized the final "s."

"It might take more than one. People have no problem equating excess with enough. It takes far longer to convince them that taking what they think they need can cause suffering for someone else. Hence the extra water."

The irony was not lost on Lila — she would have to take more than her usual share of water now in order to help everyone see that change was possible, that enough existed to flow for all. "How many stories?"

"However many it takes. Remember, we're here because I told you stories. What happened when you started sharing them?"

In a kaleidoscope of memory, Lila saw the council's careful attention around the central fire. Then her parents appeared, escorting Jacob and the other boys back from their misadventure as the village welcomed them with tears of relief and hugs. They were followed by Elena, her animated chatter as she helped Lila pack. And now here she was, sitting by a fire far from home, part of a journey that before now, she never could have imagined. She had walked for days and floated on water and Snake was here with her in the flesh, no longer confined to the space inside her mind.

Lila lifted the canteen, took a long swallow, and picked up the small reed basket.

"Come on, then, Snake. It's time for a new story."

ABOUT LAURA L. DENNIS

Laura Dennis grew up in the Finger Lakes region of New York State and is now a professor and writer in southeast Kentucky. Her work has been published in MER Vox, Change Seven, Northern Appalachia Review, Bluff & Vine, The Red Branch Review, The McNeese Review, Still: The Journal, and Bethlehem Writers Roundtable, where she was the Spring 2020 Featured Author. Her creative nonfiction received honorable mention for the 2017 Betty Gabehart Prize, she was a finalist in the 2019 Tucson Festival of Books Literary Awards, and in 2024, she signed with the University Press of Kentucky for her first book. She writes "Rural Reflections-The Reboot" on Substack and co-edits book reviews for MER. When she is not teaching, reading, or writing, she enjoys music, hiking, and spending time with her friends, family, and pets.

You can also find Laura on substack: https://lauralynnden nis3.substack.com

facebook.com/laura.dennis0371

Weep When You See Me

Parker M. O'Neill

Your dry season is nearing its end when I find the stone.

I'm walking north along one of your riverbeds, the cracked earth unrelenting underfoot. The Río Grande de Arecibo once ran all the way to your northern beaches where tourists lounged and the waters mingled, salt and fresh, like lovers' tongues. I imagine it was beautiful. Maybe it still is; maybe the beach is even prettier now so far below the poison waves. Maybe your beauty was not destroyed but merely taken from you, repurposed into silent benthic gardens where nothing lives. And you have lost so much.

A thin, trickling rope of water still runs down the arroyo's center. The river is reduced to this, or something like this, every year. Drier now than it's been in a few decades, but no one is too worried. We'll endure. And it was worse a century ago. By tomorrow the lake should be at a high enough watermark to let a little more down the river to unleash the Río Grande de Arecibo. Do you enjoy it, I wonder, when the dams open and the rains come and the waters rush across your surface like spidering veins? Out of our mountain towns, down out of the cordillera and through the looming seawalls? I imagine you like the sensation; a brush running through hair. It is this rejuvenatory tomorrow that I am picturing when I come across the stone, smooth and dusty in the red earth.

Four or five feet across, sanded down by years of rushing water into the quiet curving beauty that all river stones share. But on the stone's flattest face, upturned towards the beating sun, a series of dirt-packed indentations give me pause. On a whim I unfasten my clip from my wrist, tap the screen, and point it at the rock. Haptic feedback tells me the tool is working as I slowly pan over the river stone, and a moment later my clip's screen produces a little 3D model of the rock. I trace the dirt on the screen and mark it. My clip knows what I'm trying to do and extrapolates. Picks out the pattern I couldn't identify.

Five words: WEEP WHEN YOU SEE ME.

MY FIRST THOUGHT is that this message is from you. I envision you directing the river to eddy and swirl in such minute ways as to erode this warning into existence; or else contriving rockfalls and landslides to scrape out the letters. In my mind, you inscribed this message into a piece of yourself to warn me — but no. You work in subtler ways than this. These words were carved by desperate human hands. I'm looking through a window into the fear and decay and breaking down of the past, the heat and the droughts and the storms and the chaos and the collapse of empires.

Somewhere there's a historian in me, quieted and tamped down for so long; she's very excited. This could be a hundred years old. More. Someone placed this here; dug it into your riverbed long ago. But why?

Do you remember?

This could be a break. I haven't worked on anything like this in years. I look again at the thin string of the river trickling down the center of the dry bed. Sometimes I dream that I am the river. We ache, the river and I; it's painful to be so reduced.

I should call Acindina. She's probably worried about me. I never even told her I was going out here. But I find myself tapping my clip and dialing Eva instead.

RED SUNLIGHT POURS down in syrupy lines as I walk back. Your surface crimson-drenched; the light ruddled by smoke from the southern forests. You are no stranger to wildfires. Even before humankind left its choking, carbon mark on the world, you burned. I remember reading once that tourists used to be surprised by your weather, surprised by fire on a tropical island. To them tropical meant the hurricane. Your original inhabitants used an older form, huracan, for the fierce storms that batter you with uncertain regularity like the beat of an arrhythmic heart. But on the leeward side of the Cordillera Central, the trees are more sheltered from daily rain or huracan, sheltered enough to burn.

Do you feel diminished?

My clip buzzes. Acindina wants to talk. My heart sinks when I see her name.

"Marisol. I need to know where you are." Her voice is kind, soft. But there's an implicit demand.

"Hi. I went for a walk after work. You wouldn't believe what I found out here. I talked to Eva and she asked Hernan and it's some kind of artifact, probably from the American years, the end of them at least—"

"You talked to Eva? I've been wondering where you are for two hours. I thought you'd lost your clip, or were in trouble, or– I was worried."

It's a gut punch. "I'm sorry, Acindina," I say, autopiloting. "I didn't mean to make you anxious."

I can hear her breathing on the other end of the line, slow and regular as waves. But the ocean has risen; the waves are drowning you.

"I was worried. You said you'd tell me if you were going to go off wandering."

I wasn't wandering. But I don't want to press the issue. "It slipped my mind. I'm sorry."

Silence for a moment. Then she says, "I just thought that maybe your–that Gualtiero had found you."

"No. I'm safe." But my heart spikes at the mention of him. Odd that she should bring him up more often than I do. Maybe even being on the periphery of trauma is a kind of trauma. Or maybe scars are just more visible from the outside.

"Okay. I'm sorry, Marisol, it's just that we talked about this—"

"I know. I'll be home soon." I apologize again and we break the call. The sunset is murky through the smoke.

EVA CLIPS me a few articles about similar stones found in rivers all over your surface. I listen to them as I walk, trying to immerse myself in the history. Despite the conversation with my partner I can feel the old familiar urges pulsing, my interest in your earlier inhabitants. I want to know what the Boricuas of the past were like. I want to be involved, I want to find out more. I've been so numb.

It's called a hunger stone. The message is succinct and clear: if the water ever runs this low, beware. Stock up on what you can and be ready for hard times. Be ready for suffering. What were they thinking as they carved these words?

I want to see it in a positive light. I want to read it as a defiant act of a community in peril, spitting in the face of their troubles. In a way it's antithetical to the behavior of the ones who tried their best to ruin the world: those who proudly declared *après moi, le déluge* as things got worse for everyone else. No. Whoever cut the words into this stone wanted to help their future, even if it was too late to change things in their lifetimes.

Is the world covered in stones like this one? When the governments of the world started to falter and shatter, when the seas began to rise and the great debt owed by the empires to the workers came due, did we cover the earth in these epitaphs?

WHEN I GET BACK, Acindina's already asleep. I hesitate before shaking her shoulder. Does she really want to do this now? But I know she'd rather hear that I'm home safe. So I reach out, brushing her silky hair gently. She rises, and we sit at the kitchen table and have a cup of coffee. It's just getting dark, but her shifts start and end early; she's out of sync with your natural rhythm. An awkward ritual, corrupted by the conversation awaiting us. I watch the moon rise through the window, pale and distant, and she tells me about her day.

She's a storm tamer; a drone pilot. She controls one of the only things left on the island that emits any kind of pollution — the giant weather drones that spew their sodium cloud concoctions and turn aside the hurricanes. It's supposed to be biodegradable, after a fashion. But even if they ran on coal it might still be worth it to save ourselves from the storms.

When we first got together, I wasn't sure what to think about her job. The storm tamers have a serious training regimen in the dry season, preparing for months of readiness. And when a storm is detected, it's twenty-hour shifts until the danger is mitigated. A serious commitment to keeping the island safe, from the woman who had brought me to safety.

The storms always remind me of Gualtiero. In a way, what Acindina and I have is built on what I had with him. Salvaged from it, maybe, a harbor built out of flotsam. But how long can such a structure last?

Finally I tell her about the stone.

WEEP WHEN YOU SEE ME.

"I don't like it," she says.

"It's a piece of history. This is a chance for me to get back on track."

"How?"

"Eva talked to Hernan. They're going to remove the stone tomorrow, before the dam opens back up. They want me to come and give an interview about it."

"You think you're going to get a job just for finding it?"

"I don't know." I feel myself deflating. Drying out. "It's a step in the right direction."

"Oh, hon," she says. "I just worry you're going to backslide."

So that's what this is about. She smiles at me, worried, and I see double — the girl who saved me in the worst time of my life, and the woman who's trying to hold me back.

So much of who I am is tied up in her.

"I'm just afraid you'll lose the progress you've made," she says. "I don't think you should get involved with this. The last thing you need is to be worrying about the past, Marisol. That's not a path you want to go down."

"Why would I lose my progress?"

"It's just . . ." She swallows, looks pained. "It's like how it was when we met. You were so stressed about everything all the time. It's history, Marisol, it's not something we need to worry about right now. Let Hernan and Eva investigate it. Who cares if someone a hundred years ago carved some words into a stone? There are a thousand monuments to a thousand tragedies here. I don't want you to drown yourself in them. We can protect ourselves by looking forward, but we can't do anything about the past. It's just going to upset you again, and I want you to be happy."

"Maybe you're right," I say, but inside I know I'm just flowing with her. Taking the path of least resistance is easy; there's not so much resistance. Something about that desperate, proud stone spoke to me. I'm not happy now, I want to say. She doesn't always know best for me. Instead, we say our goodnights at the kitchen table, under the light of the cold moon, and I think of the thin stream of the Río Grande de Arecibo draining meekly into the greedy waves.

Who has shaped you?

You've been here so long. Your first inhabitants — or should I say first human inhabitants — survived off of your bounty for thousands of years. Boriken, they named you, and you were the world. But you shrunk; an empire came across the sea and the world became so much larger. I think of Gualtiero; I think of how it must have hurt you to have your beauty exploited. They named you for your precious metals. A rich port to plunder for generations. And they did; they killed and enslaved your first children and brought more slaves from across the world. How did it feel to see your earth tilled not for food but for money?

If it had ended there, you would have already seen enough suffering for a lifetime. But more always comes. The next empire did not enslave your children; so few of them were left. The world was so large then. You were lashed to the empire, made a client state. A servant, a territory. They didn't last as long as the Spanish had, but they left their mark. They did it, they said, to enrich you. To bring you into their empire. You are an island of scars, testaments to your own history: here they polluted your earth with smoking factories, here they refined oil in leaking hulking constructions along your beaches. Everywhere they poisoned the groundwater; the pharmaceutical companies too greedy to control their waste, to take proper care of you.

Why should they, they thought, when you are so small? Your greatest concerns were picayune trivialities to their ears as the world began to smolder.

And all along, the ocean; the storms, huracan to the Taíno, hurricane to the Spanish and the Americans, that wracked you. The rising tide that drowned you even as your rivers sputtered and failed. You are alone in water, choking on the detritus of empire.

JUST BEFORE I DRIFT OFF, my clip hums.

It's Eva. She wanted to make sure I was still going to come to the river in the morning. She just wants me to know that it's a big find, the first hunger stone in years, and how badly she wants me to come. There's a subtext there, like she knew I would be having second thoughts. Or that second thoughts would be forced upon me. I don't answer her.

IN MY DREAMS, I speak to you and you answer.

You take me through your peaks, your valleys; you take me into your past. I see your scars in their making.

I see the caciques ruling over their tribes. The time before the invasion. The man called Arasibo, or people's stone; the namesake of my beloved river. A chief whose brother leads the first revolt against the Spaniards.

It fails; we watch as four hundred years of pain are etched into you.

We watch the bombardment of San Juan; we see the hurricanes that devastate you again and again. You are here with me as the ocean acidifies after decades of mistreatment and the heat becomes unbearable. Together we are silent, above the peaks of the Sierra de Luquillo as the American jets and drones and helicopters move in. Their last attempt to grasp the empire slipping between their fingers, failing as soon as it begins. Soldiers throwing down their smoking weapons and begging to join us. Cowering in the craters they made.

And there runs your Arecibo, starting in the cordillera and flowing north through mountains and coffee beans and the towns sprouting alongside it. The seasonal cycles spinning before me, high watermark to low; it's dizzying to see just how much the river changes. There is the dry season low, there are the carvers leaving their mark on the hunger stone. Working out there in the arroyo with chisels in the night, hiding from the sun at the peak of the world's collapse. They had no weather drones; they had no microplastic scrubbers. They were alive in the last days of the gasoline age when nothing was guaranteed, and they didn't lose hope that there would be a future to read their message.

There are kind moments. A Taíno family sharing pieces of fruit. A quiet morning with coffee on the beach. The mist on the mountaintops.

That's what you're showing me, I realize. Time bleeds away and I see our little town, treed and green and flowering, and the river beside. The wet season follows the dry; plenty follows hunger. Acindina worries that I'm going to backslide into my old pain if I help Eva and Hernan study the hunger stone. She thinks I'll slip into who I was with Gualtiero; someone consumed by fear and hurt, someone in need of rescuing. She misunderstands. I never left that part of me behind. Your scars and my scars are always with us. I've been shaped by so many things, by Gualtiero, by Acindina. The person that I have become is informed by what has happened to me. We aren't our scars, but we can't forget them, either.

In the last moments before waking, I am your Río Grande de Arecibo and I am free, undammed, and I belong to no one.

IN THE MORNING, I stand by the banks of the riverbed as the work crew carefully pulls the stone from the dry earth. Eva and Hernan smile at me, glad I'm here, even if they don't know what I gave up by coming. But I don't feel diminished. And neither should you. You have survived the rule of two empires, one brutal and cruel; the other suffocating with false kindness, with the climate deteriorating all the while. You suffered the scars and the rising seas and never stopped protecting us. Now your surface is green and healthy; your reservoirs are cool and clear. You are Boriken, an island that is a whole world.

Acindina was wrong about the hunger stone. It isn't just a monument to a tragedy. But I think I might have been wrong about it, too. The stone is more than just a warning. Or maybe it was just a warning when it was carved, but the meaning has changed. It was placed there so long ago as a harbinger of hard times, a warning to prepare to cut rations and tighten belts. WEEP WHEN YOU SEE ME. But I don't think the words cut into the rock are what really matters anymore. We've already had the hard times — we've tamed the storms and saved our rivers and cleansed your groundwater of decades of pollution. Our belts have been tightened and loosened a hundred times, the same as you, Boriken. What the stone tells us is that there is always hope ahead. Those carvers knew someone would someday read their message, maybe even gain something from it. Even in the height of drought, even in the eye of the huracan, we can find peace in the future. No matter how many scars we bear, we can hope for freedom.

The crew finishes removing the stone and they place it, gentle as though handling a newborn, into the truck. Hernan makes a call on his clip and tells the dam operator that we're clear. Everyone cheers and they start making plans to celebrate. I tell them I'd like to stay for a few minutes and they leave, all except Eva. She sits with me on your riverbank and we watch the trickle start to grow. Soon the water is rushing, roaring, exulting in the way it tears down the arroyo and picks up dirt and dust. I think of a brush running through hair.

I think of Pico El Yunque, the proud mountaintop in your east, where your first children made carvings into the rock. Not hunger stones but depictions of the things they saw. Celebrations. There, with sharpened stones, they carved turtles and frogs into your bones. The shaman, the sun; carved under an anvil-shaped peak older than palm trees.

ABOUT PARKER M. O'NEILL

Parker M. O'Neill writes from upstate New York, where he started his creative career with a fifth grade video of the family dogs. He hopes to someday surpass that artistic high. He is a recent winner of the Elegant Literature Award for New Writers, and his fiction can be found in Apex Magazine, Flame Tree Press, Crepuscular Magazine, and elsewhere. Find his socials and some of his other work at https://linktr.ee/parkermoneill.

It Can't Be Sunday Everywhere at Once

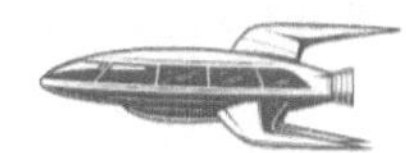

Dawn Vogel

Mirah had departed the aquatic moon of Braen with the rest of the inhabitants when the water rose high enough the Braenian government could do no more than keep the spaceport from flooding. With prayers to their god — Keasis — unanswered, and their homes sinking beneath the rising ocean, the Braenian people had sought transport on any vessel they could.

Mirah had said her goodbyes to friends and family, hoping to see them again someday, and set out for the stars.

She was glad to have a space, even if it was a single bunk and a small storage locker barely large enough to hold her salvaged belongings. The bunkroom was crowded and noisy, with someone always offering up prayers or weeping lamentations to their gods.

Two hours after the day cycle began on her second day, a severe looking woman paused in the doorway to the bunkroom. "I am looking for Mirah Galbri, she?" Her black hair pulled was back tightly, tugging her eyebrows into a perpetually surprised expression.

"That's me," Mirah said, scrambling out of her bunk and approaching the person.

"My name is Charlotte Velle, she. I've been assigned as your case worker for integration into the community of the *Skrynia*."

"Keasis's blessings to you, Ms. Velle!" Mirah dusted off her hands on her pants and extended a hand to shake.

"Charlotte, please," she replied, though without taking Mirah's hand or responding to the offer of blessings. "My first task is to find you employment. I see you have a programming background, but there are no openings in that field at present. The best I can do is get you an immediate position in tech support."

It was nothing like what she had done before, but it was a job, something to get her out of the bunkroom for a stretch of time. "Tech support sounds fine, thank you. What shifts will I be working?"

"Mid to late, seven days a week."

"Oh, there's not time off for cultural or religious observances?"

Charlotte sighed, the sound fraught with world weariness. "Standard Sunday?"

"Yes. I'm a practicing Keasian."

"I'll note it, but I can make no promises. As much as we would like to honor all requests for cultural and religious observances, if we permitted them all, the ship would no longer be able to function one day out of every seven, and that's not feasible with our timeline."

"Timeline?" Mirah echoed.

"The journey is a lengthy one, to the outer planets of the Caelestis System, where the terraforming has taken hold." Charlotte shook her head. "Only the youngest babes on the ship might someday set foot there, if they live to a venerable age. Delays decrease that likelihood."

"Oh." Mirah had heard about ships like this, ones where entire families lived and died before reaching their destination. She hadn't realized she was leaving Braen only to never set her feet on solid ground again. She had collected a jar of the soil — mud, really — from near her apartment block to bring with her on the journey, so she had a bit of Braen to anchor her prayers to Keasis. She'd hoped to mix it with the soil wherever the ship took her.

But it looked like that would never happen now.

MIRAH WASN'T SURPRISED to find the tech support role easier than her previous work.

"Most of the time, newer arrivals need help resetting their devices to Ship Standard Time," her shift supervisor, Nyst, explained. He was tall and broadly built, like someone who enjoyed playing sports or working out, hardly the sort she was accustomed to seeing in this field. But having seen the job assignment process firsthand, Mirah supposed many people ended up in places where they were needed more than they were an expert. "You walk them through that over the comms. If they have a problem you can't solve remotely, route it to a technician scheduler."

"I understand what Ship Standard Time is, but what difficulties does it present if a device doesn't correspond to it?"

"Mostly confusion for some users. If your device was still on your planet's local time, you might be late or early for your shift here, for example. Or you'd show up on the wrong day for a meeting."

As they talked, Mirah noticed the other tech support staff

hadn't had any audible interactions with any clients. "Do people message via text or voice?"

"Voice, ninety-nine percent of the time. It's just quiet some-times. We didn't take on a lot of refugees at the last stop. Just . . ." Nyst trailed off. "Well, I suppose you're among the latest, huh?"

Mirah nodded. "It'll be nice to have some quiet here. The bunkrooms have so much activity all the time."

"Oh, yeah, you get used to it, I guess. Or somehow learn to sleep through it."

"I'm sure I will. So, what do we do when we're not trou-bleshooting?"

"The terminals here have full access to the *Skrynia*'s data stores. There are reading materials, learning courses, whatever you want access to. It's all educational, of course."

"That sounds nice," Mirah said, her eyes lighting up. "Any shell environments for coding?"

"Yes, absolutely!" Nyst said, his enthusiasm matching Mirah's as he gestured to an empty terminal. "I'll show you around!"

MIRAH'S third shift fell on a Ship Standard Sunday. The comms were even quieter than normal, if that was possible.

Instead of enjoying the peace, she found herself agitated and bored. She poked through the data stores for information about the population onboard the *Skrynia* — people from eighty-three planets and moons, across five systems. The data gave numbers of people from each system, before branching off into articles about ship-born generations and the component parts of their locations of origin.

If the data for the population origins was so accessible,

Mirah wondered what else she could learn about the ship's people. Idly, she pulled up a data file regarding stated cultural origins and religious adherence within the population. From the eighty-three planets and moons onboard, there were more than two hundred different cultures represented by some portion of the ship's population, and half that number when it came to religious adherence. This article was peppered with references to Ship Standard Sunday, as well as Ship Standard Saturday and Ship Standard Wednesday as common days for religious observances across the various systems, cultures, and religions.

Mirah frowned. If she'd still been on Braen, today would have been Friday. But the ship's calendar said it was Sunday, and so it was.

She typed a new search query regarding calendars from the five systems represented in the ship's population. A ship with people from systems strewn across the cosmos likely had different calendars, with the ship's calendar derived from its system of origin. Even if half the ship's population came from that system, the odds were high the rest of the ship's population had used different calendars prior to boarding the *Skrynia*. That meant they were celebrating their holy days on Ship Standard Sunday (or Saturday or Wednesday) because that's what the calendar told them to do, even though that calendar didn't take their original calendars into account.

There was also no accounting for how the ship might calculate the long-held traditional cultural observances, which could fall on any day of the week. Mirah's shoulders slumped as she realized she'd even have to track her birthday separately from the ship's calendar if she wanted a true accounting of her age. It might have only been a number, but it mattered to her, especially since it seemed the *Skrynia* would be her home for the rest of her life.

She set her jaw. She could figure this out. Within the shell environment Nyst had walked her through, Mirah began collecting data and code from the system calendar files.

IT TOOK two weeks of data collection and code tweaking in between the sporadic service calls of her shift before Mirah was able to run her calendar comparison program. With it, she correlated the holy days for each of the religions and cultural holidays for the various planets and moons to the ship's calendar and calculated the percentage of the population that might reasonably be expected to be away from their jobs if they were given the appropriate days off as they corresponded to their home calendars. Based on the law of averages, she anticipated even spread across three potential days held as important by the myriad religions onboard, the numbers for holy days should even out to affect about one-seventh of the population on any given day. Perhaps it would be slightly higher if a particular system had a large population that all adhered to the same religious beliefs, or if several systems with large populations had matching calendars. The cultural observances were more random, but they were also less frequent.

When the numbers were done, Mirah marveled at the data's perfection, the way it reached a nearly flat line across the ship's calendar. Better yet, since not every passenger on the ship had religious beliefs, only about one-tenth of the working population on the ship would need to be given time off for religious or cultural observances on any given day, if they could be reminded their home system calendars and the ship's calendar didn't match.

Now she just had to figure out how to get this information to the people who could make changes happen.

MIRAH STARTED by requesting a meeting with Charlotte before her work shift. When she arrived, she launched immediately into talking about the work she'd done. "My research into the calendar systems in the home locations of the passengers on the *Skrynia* has indicated that the Ship Standard calendar only syncs up with the *Skrynia*'s home system."

"Yes?" Charlotte said, the skin between her eyebrows making a feeble attempt at furrowing.

"Well, I did some math alongside that, calculating which people from which systems practice which religions and have which cultural backgrounds, and only one-tenth of the workers on the ship would need any given day off if they were given the day corresponding to their religion or culture and home system's day of worship or observance."

Charlotte pressed her lips together into a tight line. "I see. But that would require adjustments throughout every department on the ship to account for numerous calendars, religions, cultural practices . . . the list goes on and on, Miss Galbri. It's not practical."

"It would just require each person to run a second calendar on their devices, and then coordinate with their department."

Charlotte shook her head. "It's clear to me you've not been in a managerial role before. There are many more hurdles to such a plan from a management perspective. They would still need to coordinate all the staffing needs and requests for time off. And when you factor in both religion and culture, it amounts to a large amount of additional work for the managers of each department. It's not something that can just magically have math and the law of averages applied to it."

Mirah frowned. "So you don't even want to see the data?"

"I don't see that it's necessary, I'm afraid."

Mirah's spirits were still low when she arrived in the tech support call center. She fiddled with the data on her tablet as she logged into her workstation.

"Hey, Mirah," Nyst said. "You alright?"

"Just a little disappointed," she admitted.

"Oh? You want to talk about it?"

Mirah glanced at her headset, then slung it around her neck so she could move it into the proper position if a call came through. "I coded up a dual calendar environment in the shell, so people from all of the systems on the *Skrynia* can practice their religious and cultural observances on the days they would if they were still where they came from. But the person I took it to didn't seem to care about it at all. She just went on about how it would be difficult for management to deal with all the requests for days off based on non-Ship Standard calendars."

"Dual calendaring, huh?" Nyst asked, pulling in a chair from an unoccupied cubicle. "Can I take a look at it?"

"Sure." Mirah passed him her tablet.

"This is really good, Mirah," Nyst said, his brow furrowed as he looked at the program on her tablet. "Whoever you took this to must not understand how easily something like this works. Your code makes this simple to just overlay this onto the calendaring system that already exists."

Mirah allowed herself a small smile at the compliment. "I based it on what the existing system used."

"Well done." He handed her tablet back.

"But it still doesn't solve anything if I can't get it implemented. I mean, we can't load this into the system without getting into trouble."

"No, definitely not. You'll need to talk to someone else about it, though. Maybe someone who's more invested in the outcome."

"Like other refugees? Start at the bottom, and work my way up?"

Nyst frowned. "I was thinking more like finding someone with the ability to take this to the ship's governmental arm, to someone who understands programming, so they see how easily this could integrate." He shrugged. "But I've only been here a few years, and I have no idea who that might be, so maybe starting by finding people who are passionate about what you're doing would help you work your way to the right person. It's worth a shot."

"Thank you. And I'm feeling much better now, so thank you for checking on me, too."

"You're welcome. I'll keep you in mind if we need to do any minor programming. Get your name on some documentation so when there's an opening elsewhere, you can fast-track into it!"

MIRAH WENT NEXT to other new refugees, her neighbors in the bunkroom. Armed with her tablet, she approached the young woman who slept on the upper bunk across from her, Elodie from Djofe, another moon in the same system as Braen.

After introducing herself to make sure Elodie recalled her name, she launched into her information. "Did you know Chagha's holy day falls on what we call Ship Standard Tuesday?"

Elodie's brow furrowed, but she nodded. "What of it?"

"Well, it seems if you wanted to appropriately practice your religion, you should have your actual holy day off from work, rather than Ship Standard Sunday."

"Be that as it may, I'm lucky if I get one Ship Standard Sunday off in a month, so I'll take what I can."

"If you put in a request for Tuesday instead—"

"Then they'd treat it like any other request for a day off, not one for religious observance. It's not the holy day the ship's calendar recognizes. And Chagha is a kind and understanding god. She won't be offended if I work on her holy day if that's what's expected in this new society."

Everywhere she went, Mirah heard a similar refrain from the newer refugees. The exact day they observed was less significant than observing something. Not working on their holy day wasn't worth jeopardizing their standing on the *Skrynia*. They were all too happy to not rock the boat, as it were.

Keasis's teachings were similar to Chagha's, and those of the gods of the other refugees. The day, the time, and even the place of worship were all adaptable. Mirah began to think she'd done all this number crunching for nothing.

But she wasn't ready to give up. She located several longer-term inhabitants who had religious titles listed alongside their names in the ship's directory and paid them visits.

The first two said they'd retired from their previous professions, keeping the titles out of habit. One was now a schoolteacher, the other worked in the ship's mess hall as a cook.

The third one, Reverend Etra, was an older woman with close-cropped white hair and a kind smile. She listened to what Mirah had to say and nodded. "You aren't the first new arrival to suggest something like this. And your experience thus far sounds a lot like mine was. But there's one difference."

Mirah was taken aback. "Oh, what's that?"

"The people within this residence block have elected me as their representative." Reverend Etra's eyes twinkled. "May I look over your work?"

Mirah handed the other woman her tablet.

Reverend Etra flipped through the pages. "This is far more elaborate and complete than the work I did five years ago."

"Five years?"

"Yes, it takes time for folks to get established here, just as if you had moved to a new city. But with this comprehensive data, I can present it to some of my colleagues, get them on our side, and bring it to a vote this time around."

Mirah gasped. "You'd do that for me?"

"Not just for you. I'd also be doing it for anyone who wants to practice their religion and celebrate their cultural and holy days unfettered by work. Even taking into consideration the permissive natures of our revered gods, the *Skrynia* demands our labor seven days a week. People deserve time for themselves, to use for religious, cultural, or even personal obligations." Reverend Etra smiled. "You came to the right person. If you can make a copy of your data, I'll start putting the right words in the right ears, and in a month or two, we should have some good news."

THREE MONTHS LATER, Nyst was helping Mirah move her sparse belongings into a recently vacated single room, when her comm pinged.

"Who's that?" Nyst asked.

"Reverend Etra." Mirah hurried into the room to place her jar of Braenian mud on a flat surface.

"Was the vote today?"

Nodding, she set the mud on the desk and read the message to herself. "It was, and the vote has passed. 'The Residential Council recommends, on behalf of all workers onboard the *Skrynia*, that workers should request the day of the ship's calendar that most closely corresponds to the cultural observance or holy day in their system of origin'. There's some more about days off for those without religious or cultural observances, so everyone can have time to rest once a week. Reverend Etra says it should just be a formality to get it officially recognized."

"So then Ship Standard Tuesday will be your day to observe your holy day, correct?" Nyst was already poking at the calendar on his own tablet.

"That's right. Oh, I can only imagine how many calls we're going to get to help people run two calendars on their personal devices, so they can track Ship Standard and their original calendars for all the non-weekly cultural observances and special holy days."

"It's not like we have much to do at work."

"I'm not complaining." Mirah grinned. "I'm looking forward to a new challenge. And Tuesdays to celebrate the many blessings Keasis has given me."

ABOUT DAWN VOGEL

Dawn Vogel has written for children, teens, and adults, spanning genres, places, and time periods. More than 100 of her stories and poems have been published by small and large presses. Her specialties include young protagonists, siblings who bicker but love each other in the end, and things in the water that want you dead. She is a member of SFWA and Codex Writers. She lives in Seattle with her awesome husband (and fellow author), Jeremy Zimmerman, and their cats. Visit her at historythatneverwas.com or on BlueSky @historyneverwas.

The Sculptor

Ezra Wu

Greatness takes many paths in art. But every path leaves, not one masterpiece, but a series, a reflection of the life that created them. Great artists dedicate a lifetime to their work.

But there is a separate greatness in art, one that demands not merely a lifetime, but a *life*.

My own lifetime in the world of art has put me in a position to see many talented young artists pass through on their own paths to greatness. In such a position, it is my responsibility to recognize this greatness and propel it forward through my connections and experience.

But I do, on rare occasions, see greatness as it follows this secret, hidden path. And, in vain, I urge these cursed souls to follow any other.

EARLY IN MY CAREER, I scrounged an income by working part time as an instructor under a mentor of mine. Gretta was a talented painter but taught all varieties of media, her skill as an instructor more key than any artistic specialty. One summer, the necessities of rent found me assisting with Gretta's intermediate sculpting class.

Considerable assistance was required. Few students had worked with anything other than clay, and even soapstone was not so easily shaped. There were plenty of children to console about irreparable mistakes, adults to cajole into making their first irreversible cuts. All in all entertaining, if tedious.

We made it through the hour. The soapstone shapes were shunted off into a corner of the crowded classroom. As Gretta handled the last of the students, I inspected the aggregate of them, trying to guess which of whose creators we would be seeing again and which would never return.

One last student came by to drop off her work. Not one I had seen in any of Gretta's other classes, nor had she been one of the many students clamoring for my attention earlier.

She held her piece in front of her with two hands, almost as if she were hiding it — but not quite.

"How did it go?" I asked.

She shrugged. "It didn't turn out how I wanted it to."

"Well, it looks like that was the case for most of the class. Mistakes are inevitable. It's just a matter of learning how to adapt to them."

She frowned, still holding her fist full of soapstone in front of her.

"At the beginning of class," she said, "Ms. Gretta said that sculpting is finding the shape within the stone, then making it free. But if you make a mistake, then you're not making the stone's shape anymore. You're making the shape of your mistakes."

She looked awfully young — she was at an age where her

peers went to great pains to make themselves look older, and her lack of participation only highlighted her youth. Her appearance was unremarkable but, even frustrated and exhausted as she was, her eyes were set with determination.

"Well, maybe the stone meant for you to make those mistakes," I said at last.

She cracked the barest of smiles, not unlike unearthing a sliver of sculpture from a block of stone.

"Maybe. But I think the stone probably wouldn't have asked someone like Ms. Gretta to make so many mistakes."

I smiled too. "Well, there's nothing for it. You'll just have to keep practicing. Why don't you drop off what you've got so far? Next class you'll be polishing and finishing them."

She nodded and carefully deposited her work onto the bench. As she let go, the soft stone made an extended clatter, which confused me at first. But then she pulled her hands away and smiled sheepishly.

She had broken it into smaller chunks, the smallest barely more than a cubic inch. Each, it seemed, was the careful excision of some mistake in an attempt to return to an unsullied block.

She left before I could comment on her unusual approach. I looked back down to her scatter of stone. Picking one up, I saw she had at least tried to work a little more with the mistake she had removed.

"That's Elise's, isn't it?" said Gretta, finally free from the crowd of students. "She's odd, isn't she? Probably the most talented person in this class. Including me, at least when it comes to this 3D stuff."

I was still rummaging around her little blocks of stone, inspecting each in turn.

"How old is she?" I asked idly.

"Fourteen. Just started high school. I thought I'd try to convince her parents to send her to a school with a good program, give her a head start for college. There's only so much I can do, after all. I can teach her the craft, but she needs a real mentor to teach her the art."

"That good, huh?"

"And she's dedicated, too. Apparently, she spends all her allowance on supplies."

"Well, at least she's passionate," I said. "Persistence is something else."

Gretta grinned. "I'm sure she has that too."

She took one of Elise's sculpturettes and held it out for me to inspect.

Its shape was unmistakable. A human ear, impossibly delicate for such soft and low-quality soapstone. She had carved the shell of the ear around the stone's sole patch of spidery veins, just where the skin might be thin enough to show the vessels beneath.

I looked at the other fragments of her block with new eyes, seeing now the rough shape of the ear, or where trying to carve some unusual curve had split the stone. She must have attempted that single ear four or five times on increasingly smaller pieces of stone until, at last, perfecting it on a sliver of stone the size of a large coin.

"She'd probably have kept going if she could," said Gretta. "But unlike most perfectionists, she does accept there are limits to what she can actually achieve."

"For now," I said.

Gretta nodded her agreement and replaced the ear amongst its predecessors.

"For now."

THAT WAS the last I saw of Elise for several years, which was not surprising. I only spent a few months in Gretta's classroom. My commissions began to pick up, and the credibility that is so highly valued in our small world increased with them. Just as I began to be able to support myself off art alone, I received an offer for a position of artist-in-residence for a local college. I accepted.

I was attending the final show of the year for some of my friends in the student body when I saw her again. It was a bit of an awkward dance. Our eyes met, but she seemed uncertain whether she recognized me, and while I remembered her quite well, she was much changed.

"Were you one of Gretta Lamberg's students, maybe four years ago?" I ventured.

Recognition found her at last. "I was. You taught a few classes, didn't you? My name's Elise Smith."

"Avery Lehrer. What are you studying?" I asked, already knowing the answer.

"Sculpture," she said.

"Of course," I replied. "Are you showing your work here today?"

She nodded. "It's over there, in the back."

She turned towards the back of the room, and was quickly swallowed into the crowd. I paused a moment before following her.

It was not just age that had changed her since I'd seen her last. Then, she had been mostly unremarkable in appearance, same-ish in the way children are. She was remarkable now. But not beautiful. No, more the opposite. Something was changing beneath her skin, as if some thought occupied her mind with such frequency that it had begun to push through to shape the face around it.

She was not beautiful, but all the same, I found it impossible to look away.

First year students were allowed little more than a desk's worth of space for their work. For sculpture students, this was probably just one piece, maybe two at best. I was a little amused to see Elise's elections were both smaller and more numerous than her peers. I imagined that I could see echoes of that soapstone ear in the four pieces she had chosen: an ankle frozen in tension carved from knotted wood, a cast of an indistinct silhouette entwined around itself. She had since branched out from the human form as well: from found materials a bristling array of fangs, a texture of stone that blended seamlessly from rough fur to wrinkled skin, like one might find on the corners of a smiling mouth.

Each piece was simply titled "Study" followed by a number. Unlike her classmates, she had elected not to provide some commentary about the work, and instead had provided a summary of the assignment they had been created for.

It attracted little attention, though I caught murmurs of approval from those who walked past. Others might have seized the opportunity to engage the commenters, but Elise was unconcerned, almost bored.

"How have classes been?" I asked.

"Good," she said. "They keep me busy. More than I'd like."

"There's something else you'd rather work on?" I guessed.

She nodded. "Though I do see the use of them. Things like the maw—" she gestured to the spikes of glass teeth "—are still useful, even if I'm just going to throw it out later. The sculpture makes me as much as I make the sculpture, after all. Now that I think of it, you told me that, didn't you?"

"I might have said something to that effect," I said, dubiously. "Are you really going to throw it away?"

"I don't exactly have the space to keep it," she said.

"Why not sell it?"

Elise looked over to her classmates, speaking with much

animation to the visitors of their mini exhibitions — potential buyers, connections, patrons.

"They're deluding themselves," she said. "No one's interested in buying assignments from a first-year student at a mediocre art school."

"But you won't be a student forever," I replied. "And I think you can expect more than mediocrity, unlike some people." I tried not to look too meaningfully towards her neighbor's work.

"Well, thank you. I suppose that's kind of you to say. But I have my own expectations of myself, and they have little to do with whether or not someone thinks it's a good investment to buy my first-year art projects."

"Very true," I said. "Something that's easy to forget, I imagine. You and I should stay in touch. I'm here for a while as an artist-in-residence. And yourself?"

"My program has another three years. I expect I'll stay for most of it."

"I'll make sure to make some time soon, then. Before you move on to bigger and better things."

She smiled, a little uncomfortably. "I was surprised to see you again, but pleased. Do you see Ms. Gretta much anymore?"

"We grab lunch every so often."

"I hadn't thought about her in ages. Can you give her my thanks, and my apologies? I always meant to visit."

"I can. I'll see you soon, Elise."

"I HEARD you were awarded the Gallagher's Prize. Congratulations."

"That was last year," Elise said evenly, staring out over the city. Our park of choice overlooked the city's modest Main

Street, fairly busy on a weekend morning. Around Elise, the bustle of the city was muted, further away than it actually was.

"Well, I hadn't seen you since then. You're awfully hard to get a hold of."

"You know where to find me."

"I don't like to interrupt while you're at the studio."

"Hm. Well, I appreciate it. I wish others would be as considerate."

"You mean Dr. Delaney? You could return the consideration. He wouldn't interrupt trivially. Those dinners and shows are important opportunities."

"Opportunities?" she said. "For what?"

"For your future as an artist. You're right, you know. No one's interested in the art of a second-year student. You're getting to the point where talent matters less and less. People want to know where you're headed as an artist. Titling every work 'Study X' or 'Experiment Y' tells them nothing about you as an artist, and where it will take your career."

Elise blinked blearily, then let out a snort of laughter.

"What?" I asked. "Did I say something?"

"No. Yes. It just never occurred to me to make a career out of this."

"Really?" I was flabbergasted. "Then why — what are you doing here? What's the point?"

Elise leant over the railing. "There's something important I have to make. Something important I have to say. And this is the only way I can say it. As I am now, it won't be expressed the way it needs to be. But I don't mind if it takes me years, hundreds of attempts, thousands of dollars. One day, I'll have it. That's all that matters."

It was like the moment with the ear, all those years ago. The mundane titles, the unfinished works she was becoming notorious for. Her lack of interest in the social ladder that would foster her as she progressed. Not even considering a career!

What was my reaction then? I suppose I must have thought her tragically naive. But I was also impressed. With any other young artist I might have dismissed the idea as outlandish or idiotically romantic. But from Elise, I could believe it.

"So, then, this magnum opus of yours. How long have you been working on it?"

"Since before I met you. Before I met Gretta, even."

"And every study, every exercise and assignment, was all in service of it?"

"It was a stretch for some of them. But as best I could, yes."

I began to filter through my memory of every piece she had made. Sculptures, sketches, even essays. Putting them together was difficult, but suggested something strange, grotesque, exhilarating.

"Then everything — it's all been pieces of it. How does it all fit together? How close are you to having the whole thing?"

Elise's eyes lit up. "Nothing's set in stone. Not yet. But every day it becomes clearer, and I become more capable of it. I have sketches, notes. I, uh, keep them in my room. I don't want the others to see them. But I could show you, if you like."

I accepted her offer. The sketches were as strange and fascinating as I had dreamed they were, as beautiful and awesome as their creator herself.

ELISE LEFT her program within the year. Only somewhat coincidentally, my artist-in-residence program was completed as well, and I accepted a teaching post across the country. But there were several months remaining before I needed to begin my work, so I spent them on my own art and catching up with neglected friends and connections. Elise included.

It was a long drive up to the tiny town she had chosen to

make her new home. A longer journey than I would have even entertained for anyone else, but I had a feeling this might be the last opportunity to see her for a long while.

I arrived early in the evening. The town could barely be called such: a single street, woven between tall cliff faces of stone, glowing blue in the evening light. Small houses, some carefully maintained, others long since fallen into disrepair, faded gradually into a handful of quaint storefronts and restaurants. I found the address Elise had given me and parked outside. From where I stood I could see the end of the town, the hills and forests beyond.

A door opened across the street, the only movement in the entire town. In the half dark I could make out a silhouette.

"Elise! It's good to see you again."

Elise stepped out from the shadow of her doorway.

She had changed yet again. There was no way to look at her and see the same girl I had met ten years before. Even the young woman I had met again at University was difficult to find within this new countenance. The evolving thing I had caught a glimpse of all those years ago had taken over, reshaped the face that housed it. Hollowed it out and began to fill it with something new.

Yet, she was somehow just as entrancing as when I had seen her last.

"I'm a little in disbelief that you're really here. That you came all this way," she said as she helped me gather my belongings from the car. She struggled with them, more than I would have expected.

"It's always nice to have a change of scenery," I said. "It's beautiful here, though very difficult to get to."

"The two aren't unrelated," she said with a hint of a sigh.

Elise's entryway was dark, though I could see warm yellow lights flicker in an adjacent room — her studio, no doubt.

She felt along the walls for the lights to the hallways,

kitchen, living room. Most surfaces I saw were covered in an appreciable amount of dust. As spacious as her home was, she seemed to have little use for it.

Elise rummaged around in her kitchen with some annoyance.

"I meant to have something made for you as you arrived, but I lost track of time . . . It happens more often than not these days."

Elise's pantry was freshly stocked. Flustered, she shuffled through its contents, muttering as she attempted to recall the recipes she had intended them for.

"Would you like some assistance?" I offered.

"I don't usually — on my own I don't really bother, but—"

"I'll help you out," I said smoothly.

Elise accepted my direction with palpable relief. Together we made a basic meal of roasted fish and vegetables. I was grateful for the simple activity to break the ice between us.

Elise served me first, then herself. She sat across from me and ate as I did.

She bit into it slowly, frowning.

"Does it taste okay?" I asked. I was barely more of a cook than her.

"It tastes . . . good. Better than anything I've had in a long time."

She ate with relish. Our meal passed with few words, both of us too hungry to talk. I, from my day of driving, and she, apparently from something else.

At last, when the food was gone, conversation could not be put off any longer. Elise cleaned the plates and dusted off the ancient couches she had clearly inherited from the home's previous owner.

"How have you been Elise, since I saw you last?"

"Fine," she said. "Leaving the program was the right choice.

It was becoming hard to make time for my commitments to my classes. There are much fewer distractions here."

"Not much at all."

Elise smiled. "No. But there are quarries. Artist grade marble. And it's significantly cheaper if you don't have to pay for it to be transported across the country. They're just over the hill. I can show you in the morning, if you'd like."

"Sure," I replied. "Do you visit them often?"

Elise shrugged. "Normally, no. There's a stone yard in town. I can see the pieces there."

"Do you have many friends in town?"

"They've come to expect me in the shops."

There was little more to be said on that matter. The real question, the one I had come all this way to ask, was all that was left.

"Elise, how is your work going? Are you still making progress?"

She nodded. "It's slow, but as steady as always." Her hands flitted along the hem of her shirt. "It's all becoming much more concrete now. These are the tools that I'll use, the stone I'll carve it from—"

"You're close then? Will you let me see? Your studio's in the back, isn't it—"

I surprised myself with my own eagerness. I was on my feet before I even realized it. I might have run towards the back, towards the warm light still shining there, if Elise's expression of terror had not stopped me.

"Wait, I've—" Her voice shook. "I've already started — tried to start, several times. The start of it, it's still in there, but I don't want anyone to see it. Not yet. I . . . don't know if I want anyone to see it at all."

The artistic force and the body that contained it were at war then. It was easy for me to forget that she was not just her artistic ambitions, but it was even easier for Elise herself. Easier not to remember she was only just an adult, living alone for the first time, far from everything she had ever known. Her dedication fortified her against it, but at the same time, it was what had brought her here in the first place.

She held her hands over her face. "I'm beginning to wonder how I'll know whether it will be time, if it will ever—"

I grabbed her shoulder and sat down beside her on the dust-ridden couch.

"It's a marathon, Elise. Not a sprint. You need to look after yourself. Clean this place up, get to know your neighbors. Exercise, feed yourself properly. Find a life for yourself outside your art."

Elise shook her head. "My life *is* my art."

The petulance of that statement cracked a smile in Elise that staved off the tears.

"If your life is your art then take good care of it. Stone is hard work. You can't do it on an empty stomach."

"You're right, of course," she said, rubbing her eyes with her sleeves, though I had not seen any tears. "I'll clear out my studio tomorrow morning, move the attempts out so I can show you the studies at least."

"Why not move the studies out here instead? I think your main room was meant to be a storefront anyways."

She frowned. "You mean, to sell them?"

"If there are any you can part with."

"There are plenty, but I'd rather not spend the time."

"Price them low enough and they'll sell themselves. What would you do with them otherwise?"

"Not much," she admitted.

"Something is better than nothing. It will also build good-will with your neighbors. I can help you get set up while I'm here."

She seemed not to know how to respond to my generosity.

"I'm exhausted," she said at last. "Let's discuss this more in the morning, perhaps on our walk to the quarry. You can take my room, down the hall."

"What about you?"

"I've been sleeping in my studio lately."

I DID INDEED HELP Elise set up a small shop. There were maybe twenty or thirty pieces she judged acceptable for the townspeople to peruse or purchase, all of them artistically intriguing in their own right, but all obviously and tantalizingly unfinished.

We sold them more quickly than expected. The townsfolk were curious about the newcomer, and Elise's art was extremely generously priced. I commented that she would be out within the month at this rate. She replied she had more pieces, but those could not be shown, much less sold. Even to me.

Did I ever see her first attempts at the final work? I will be honest, if there had been an opportunity, I would have taken it. But there were none. Perhaps knowing this, Elise and I spent nearly every moment of those few days together. She continued to spend nights in her studio, preventing me from stealing a glance while she slept.

But she did show me new sketches, new studies and practices. And as before they were magnetic, and spoke powerfully of the work that was to come.

AGAIN, I did not see Elise for several years. My own career took off, then plateaued, but not in a way that was undesirable to me. My place within the community solidified itself in a position of mentorship and also recognition of rising talent. A stable career allowed me to stabilize other aspects of my life: I bought a house, started a family. I thought rarely of Elise, but when I did, I wondered about the differences between the nature of her happiness and mine, and whether one could ever come to appreciate that of the other.

It was a rare night alone. My partner had taken our son for a weekend trip while I was unexpectedly detained with work. Our house was quiet and oddly cold, and I was listless.

The phone rang. I did not recognize the number.

Normally I would not have answered, but some compulsion bade me to. Another opposing one bade me not. As I hovered in indecision over the phone, the answering machine made it for me.

"Avery, this is Elise.

"It's . . . almost done. It happened so much more quickly than I thought. So many failed attempts, so much struggle, but . . . it's all fallen away. Within the month, Avery, it will be complete.

"I . . . I'm not sure that I want it to be."

The message ended. I immediately tried to call her back. She did not answer. The same when I called the next morning, and the next.

SUCH WAS the state of my life that the month Elise had promised had come and gone and I still had not made time to go see her. Between obligations to my students and my family I had only just begun to find time to seek her out when news of her reached me first.

The conversation occurred at the end of year student show — an important time to seek out connections, patronage, as talented young artists sought ways to transition from these shallower shores. Conversation should have been dominated by discussion of the merits of students' work. Instead, in a secretive whisper, spreading through the crowds like wildfire—

"Everyone I know from the state has gone to see it already. Further south, my old professor says they're arranging transportation for the whole faculty—"

"She's refused all offers to have it shown at any gallery, refuses even to move it from that tiny town of hers. A four-hour drive from the nearest airport, but still people are going in droves—"

"—can't get a straight explanation from them. But they say it's the most remarkable work of the decade, maybe the century! We'll have to see for ourselves—"

"It smells of a scam, or a hoax. But old Sakwood was smitten. He wouldn't have fallen for that kind of trick—"

"—a nobody. At least, previously. Won a few awards, dropped out of Barton's... Say, didn't Professor Lehrer use to work there?"

"Say, Avery, you wouldn't happen to recognize the name Elise Smith?"

"I do," I said coolly. "Our time at Barton's overlapped. She was well known as a talented student. I'm not surprised to hear of her success."

The murmurs exploded into unabashed interest then. I was bombarded with questions: What was her art like? What motivated her? What kind of person was she? Could I convince her to come as a speaker?

I answered all questions dimly, without detail. Both out of respect for Elise and her reclusive nature, but also because there was no other answer I could provide. Not until I went to see the sculpture for myself.

I HAVE NEVER since experienced anything like it. There is a certain quiet often found in art museums and galleries, a certain sobriety born of respect both for the art and the appreciation of it. What occurred in Elise's gallery went far beyond it. The gallery, packed as it was, was still. The silence bordered on reverence.

Could I describe it? Only in terms of my reaction to it. Any other attempt would fall short. To say it was beautiful would be untrue. To say it was hideous, untrue as well. Graceful, brutal. Intricate, violent. Imposing, intimate. Emotional, yet lifeless as stone. One could exhaust the entirety of human language trying to describe it and not yet manage to catch what Elise had made real in marble.

I recognized it as soon as I saw it, not from Elise's sketches or her studies, but from Elise herself. This was the vision that had shaped her, now made manifest. What had previously lingered beneath the skin, haunted the hollows of her eyes, had now emerged. And it was more than I could ever have imagined.

I wept to see it. I was not the only one. To gaze upon it emptied my heart of all previous loves and despairs and filled it with something else entirely.

At the gallery's closing, I and the other occupants were dumped in a daze onto the cold streets. Once the shock had faded, the crowds were clamoring to see the artist. Where was Elise Smith? Who was she? Could she be met?

The shopkeeper next door, who Elise had apparently hired to see to her gallery in the months prior to the completion of her work, explained that Elise would not be seeing any visitors, and expressed her preference that he not share her location with anyone else. His small-town loyalty stood strong against appeals to fame, threats of violence, even bribes. The crowd dismissed itself in dejection, but showed every sign of returning the next day.

I stayed behind. The shopkeeper recognized me from the few days I had spent here years ago, and when I asked, he admitted that Elise was still in town. When I asked if I might see her, he frowned and said that her answer might change for me but it seemed unlikely.

I asked if he at least knew if she was alright.

"Hard to say," he said. "I never knew her to do anything but work on that sculpture of hers."

"And now it's done," I said.

I STAYED in that tiny town for several days, hoping that each would be the day I could see her. I was not the only one.

The crowds swelled as word spread. The town became a circus of feuding artistic egos all demanding her attention, making greater and greater offers in an attempt to cajole her to appear. Luckily, such theatrics did not extend beyond the streets outside: Elise's gallery was left in reverent silence. I began to spend more and more of my time there, content to spend hours lost in the mastery of Elise's creation.

One night, allowed to stay a little later on my own by the shopkeeper, the door to the back of Elise's studio unlocked with a quiet click. A few moments later, it swung open, silently.

Soft footsteps approached me. The bench I sat on shifted as it took on another's weight.

"Elise," I said, unable to look away from the sculpture.

I heard the small sounds of a presence beside me — breathing, rustling cloth. The bench creaked ever so slightly as she shifted beside me.

"It's done," she said. "The work of a lifetime, complete in only half that."

"How does it feel?" I asked, eyes still lost among the sculpture's surfaces. "To be done, at last?"

"I haven't decided yet," she said.

"Are you not happy with it?"

"The sculpture? No, it's exactly as I dreamed of. And at once, so much more. But to have finished it. I don't know that I ever thought that far ahead."

In some ways, neither had I. I always imagined Elise's work to be finished as she neared her deathbed, for her to collapse as she completed the final detail. To see her completed work for the first time just as the life left her eyes. Cliche, I know, but how else was a work of such ambition and scope to be completed, if not by the hand of eternity itself?

I realized though, that it was not too late for her to enact such an ending.

"What comes next, Avery?" I heard her say.

The gallery was still and cold. Our voices did little to lift the weight of that silence.

"I suppose you rest on your laurels, for now," I said. "There are very many people who would assist you with that."

Outside, we could just barely hear two blustery curators attempt to one-up the other with what they would offer the sculpture's creator for a chance to show it in their venues. Elise snorted her disdain.

"You know I've never cared about those things."

"Because it distracted you from your work," I said. "But now it's done. What harm could it do?"

She sighed. "I suppose you're right, as always. I'll see you tomorrow, Avery."

And with that, she stood up from beside me and left as quietly as she had come.

THE NEXT MORNING, as I and the latest arrivals came to see the sculpture, there was someone waiting for us in the small foyer before Elise's gallery. She stood at the gallery's entrance, her back towards us as she gazed into the sculpture room.

"Excuse me," said the head of the crowd. "You wouldn't happen to be—"

She turned around. There was a collective gasp. Even though I knew what to expect, I am ashamed to say that within it was my own.

There had been a question in my mind. Now that the vision haunting her every waking thought was real, would it let her go? Would she regain what she had before it had seized hold of her so firmly? Was she free at last?

But I was wrong. The question was meaningless. Because there was no vision, and no Elise. The vision *was* Elise. Like a photonegative, or a mold to a cast, one could not produce a work of such magnitude without also remaking oneself. Just as she had spent years persuading stone to take her shape, the stone, in its own way, had achieved the same from the flesh around her.

"I am Elise Smith. Thank you all very much for attending my gallery."

Her admirers were ecstatic. Credit to human nature, truly we can adapt to anything. They were only momentarily taken aback by the strangeness of her countenance, as indescribable as her sculpture. They swamped her in a flood of offers — famous venues, prestigious positions, frankly absurd amounts of money. Elise politely informed them that neither she nor her work would be leaving the valley, and the sculpture was absolutely not for sale.

In the end, Elise accepted a modest title of 'Artist Fellow' from a similarly modest institution. A banquet was held in her honor in the town's largest restaurant, attended by the institution's president and the faculty of the fine art department. It was a somber affair. All its participants were mellowed by the quiet that followed both Elise and her creation, as well as all that looked upon them.

I flew back home to my partner and child. All in all, this might have been a happily ever after.

I HAD some connections at Elise's institution. One of the responsibilities of her position was to compose monthly letters on the nature of both her work and on art as a whole. They informed me that these letters had grown increasingly erratic, before coming to a stop altogether.

Worried, a colleague of mine sent an excerpt from her last letter.

"On the Purpose of Art.

"The purpose of art is a pointlessly contentious question. To those of us who create it, art is its own purpose. This is a truth felt deep within us, incontrovertible as existence itself.

"But perspectives exist outside our own. Evolutionarily, we invest time and resources on an exercise not directly related to survival to demonstrate fitness to prospective mates. More directly, we use art to communicate problems and solutions both internal and external. Personal reasons often fall neatly into these two categories: desire for fame and wealth, the first. Activism fits into the second.

"But I, and perhaps you, find a third motivation. An urge that exists beyond even yourself, to make real an inexpressible truth, a

phenomena of brain and heart and soul that withers and turns to ash when made bare to the harshness of the world around us.

"Art, then, is the twisting, the bending of the material, to make real what cannot be. Art is the balance of the adulteration of the existence within such that it can exist without, but not so much that the truth of that existence is lost. Art is to challenge the impossibility of this task. Art is to succeed.

"But even then, success is not enough. To take this fragile thing and give it a body of stone still leaves it weak. Even when the transmission of artistic truth is perfect, the stone will one day crumble. A body of stone lasts only a little longer than bone and flesh. Why is it that to be real is to be finite, to be limited? Why is non-existence — death — the only infinity we can touch?

"This, I suppose, is the price we pay to bless this world with but a moment of expression. And we must be content with knowing that the inexpressible continues on, past when bones and stone alike turn to dust."

I SHOWED my partner Elise's letter. My better half knew that to ask for advice meant my heart was unsteady for reasons my mind could not find. With the blessing of my family, I flew back to Elise with resolve. These are the things that fortify the soul against the uncertainties it finds in life.

True to her word, Elise had not left her town since her arrival. But years had passed. The circus that had once filled her tiny town had long since moved away. It had reclaimed its solitude, perhaps too eagerly — quiet and stolid had passed forth into disrepair and decay.

I knocked twice on Elise's door. It rattled on its hinges. The entire townhouse groaned and complained.

Elise opened the door and stepped outside of the doorway, head bowed.

"Avery—"

The halls were dark behind her, but in the gloom I could see the door to her gallery, barricaded shut. A bookshelf had been pushed against it, scraps and supplies piled around it.

"Elise, are you alright? Why have you shut your gallery? Is the sculpture still—"

Elise's shoulders began to shake.

"You came to see me, didn't you? All those years, it was me, wasn't it? I'm here, aren't I. You don't need to go there, you don't..."

Elise was only moments away from sobs. Even in the darkest moments of the sculpture's creation I had never seen her so distraught.

I pushed past her, and she flinched. But then I pulled the door shut behind her, and she looked up at me in shock.

"Let's go for a walk then, shall we?"

Elise hesitated on her doorstep, then stepped off carefully, as if she had not left for a long, long time.

It was early evening, and the fading sun gave way to the dim glow from the lights of the homes along the way. The town was quiet, save for the sound of wind through the empty streets and the trees in the cliffs above them.

I had no destination in mind, but there were few places to wander within the town. Before long we found ourselves outside the quarry's stone yard. Elise pulled open the chain around its gate and let herself in.

The stone yard was bright despite the darkening evening. Huge blocks of marble, stacked atop each other two or three high, collected what was left of the blue light and threw it across the yard's winding paths. Elise seemed at ease here, running her fingers along the surfaces of rough stone.

I quickly lost track of which paths we had taken. My sense of direction followed soon after. The tall stone walls cut off any sight of the town, the trees. Even the wind was lost, wandering the paths in disoriented blusters. Elise was unperturbed and walked the labyrinth with familiarity.

She stopped, perhaps at the stone yard's center, perhaps not. There was a small clearing here, where several stone blocks had been shifted, taken or toppled over.

"I spent hours here, even before I had begun. Looking for the shape within the stone. For how that shape would shape me."

She lifted her hand, as if reaching out to trace a memory of something which was no longer there.

"You found it, didn't you? Your sculpture, it's . . ." Words failed to describe it, as always.

"Yes, I did. The moment was magical. Like love at first sight." She smiled sadly. "But also, a vision of the end, into eternity itself.

"Avery, in my mind . . . I began to confuse us, the sculpture, myself. What was the difference? Flesh, stone, the medium means nothing. All my life I have labored as hard to create the sculpture as I have to make myself worthy of it. And now there are two of us. And she is so much more than I am, than I will ever be. What is the point then, of me, now that I have her to take my place? What more could I want? What more could I even ask for?"

The wind rose with the coming of night. No stars, no moon, yet still the marble glowed with its own internal light. Elise's shoulders shook silently, and I had the strange thought that she might be laughing.

"You've tried for years to find the part of me that is not her. And I've gone through the motions, but I never found anything, Avery. There's nothing there."

Elise fell to her knees, surrounded on all sides by heavy stone. I was spell struck and found it impossible to approach her.

But I had to nonetheless. With every step as heavy as lead, I walked over to her. I fell to my knees, took her face in my hand.

"You have to make a second one, Elise."

She stared back at me, eyes wide and startled.

"I can't," she said. "She is all I ever had. I have nothing left."

"Then find something. Make something from nothing. It's what artists do. You—"

"I'm not an artist, Avery, I'm—"

"You don't have a choice, Elise! There's no other way. Make a second sculpture, then a third. Do it again and again. Prove to yourself that there's more to you than that sculpture, even if it's just another one. It's the only way."

I could see Elise struggle with the idea, face contorting as she tried to make sense of it. To envision how a life devoted to one monumental task could be reformed to take on another.

"It seems impossible that I would ever be free of her," she said at last.

It was well and truly night now. The glow of the stones no longer seemed to defy the darkness, and though the stone yard was darker for it, it was somehow more navigable.

"You have to try. If you have nothing left, then you have nothing to lose."

Dear Avery,

I hope this letter finds you well. I have news, either good or bad. It depends on your point of view.

Work continues on my second sculpture, but I can already tell, it is a failure. After years of work, it grows day by day more complete, and more apparent that it will never be a worthy successor to the first. I know already, what the first is, the second will never be.

Avery, it is the first time in my life that I have met failure. Doubt, struggle, even despair, I know them well. But all these were in service of an ultimate triumph, which steeled me against them. Failure has a finality that I had never expected to confront, perhaps even feared. But now, as I rapidly approach it, I realize I have found a new perspective on what I've had, and what I've lost.

My life has been defined by a purpose, and while it was unmet, I could not understand it. But now that it has abandoned me, I can feel its shape in the hollow it has left, in the cracks that it rent in its departure.

Consumed by it, I felt it as a desire for existence. Puzzling now, as I look back on it, as its existence was indisputable, both within and indistinguishable from my own. So if existence was not enough, then what was? Not simply to be made physical, as physicality is only one illusion among many. Not immortality, for stone too will one day crumble. Not fame, not fortune, all those things I eschewed in its pursuit. Then what was the nature of the desire that consumed me so powerfully, and without understanding, I somehow achieved?

The answer, I believe, is to exist within the minds of others. Or, in other words, to be understood. The transmission of an idea, perfect and uncolored by the mind that receives it. The power of the idea demanded it, the power of the idea allowed it to be achieved. And then, once it had, what to do with the shell that had birthed it, now so redundant and lost?

You and I, we thought that another sculpture might set me free, that the creation of a second might shape me just as the first had, and somehow, I might become more than it. But I was not shaped by my creation, any more than it was shaped by me. She and I found ourselves in this world and shaped it until we found a way to exist. The second sculpture has no such existence, and will never exert itself in the same way. Yet still, I continue to work. Even though to me it seems like food without taste, words without meaning, life without art.

Because, I've realized, this absence — maybe it's not important. This sculpture means little more to me than all the sketches and studies I've created and discarded over the years. They served their purpose and I never thought of them again. But they persist, and some, even, are treasured. My neighbors effuse admiration, my teachers display them proudly in their homes, my parents send me photos of trinkets I had long since forgotten. They mean nothing to me, yet somehow they have become something to everyone else. Somehow, something is created by this imperfect transmission. Something real.

I have made a thousand people witness to what lives inside me, a thousand people have been made to understand what I am. But these people, I don't understand any of them, not at all. And why do I deserve to live on, while those thousands in whom I reside — more compassionate, more complete — shall perish?

Avery, I write to inform you that I have destroyed the sculpture. I know this is unthinkable to you, but you could not have stopped me: I am soon to follow. My health is failing, slowly enough that I still hope to finish this second sculpture, but surely enough that the end is in sight. There is little I will leave in this world, but the sculpture . . . its shadow is too heavy for what little else there is. It bears so much of me — my ambitions, my weaknesses, my despair — that otherwise I cannot imagine I will ever be left in peace. At one time that might have been what I wanted, but now I am not so sure. Rather, if I live on only as a memory, if I entrust my existence to those who knew me, whether I am loved or forgotten, I feel as though I might at last be content.

YOURS, *truly.*
Elise Smith

ENCLOSED with the letter was a fragment of stone in the shape of a human ear, so exquisitely textured that, warming in my hands, it seemed as soft as skin.

ABOUT EZRA WU

Ezra Wu writes, draws, and makes games. They're the latest in a long line to wonder if fiction can change the world, and they're using their own blood, bones, and brains to find out. You can find their work at https://nebulos.space, as well as in a small but growing variety of less guerilla publications.

Hardly Working

Christoper R. Muscato

Work was vital and good. Like any good, productive member of society, Paul lived by this mantra. It was the creed by which he set his routines, how he had raised his children, how he estimated his own value. And there was plenty of work to do. New vertical greenhouses were being built. Land needed rewilding. Recycling stations overflowed with refuse waiting to be converted into new products. Wind farms needed maintenance, tidal turbines required monitoring, and the old infrastructure had to be dismantled. And that didn't even account for the construction of stormproof shelters, or all the coding and programming that went into consolidating the new power grid.

Green thumbs do not grow on idle hands, as the saying went.

Paul stretched out his back, felt the series of pops. Pain was a part of life. Inevitable. He wore it like a badge of honor, a testament to all the labor he had completed in his 68 years. It was proof he was productive, and that he had never given in to that parasitic temptation to let his labor be assumed by machines.

Paul glowered at the thought, and shoved his hands back into the mulch he was sorting.

That task finished, Paul worked through the corridors of his vertical greenhouse, pushing past leafy curtains so thick it was impossible to see more than a few feet ahead. Green things needed to grow, and here, they achieved it.

Shoving through a wall of rutabaga leaves as broad as his head, Paul arrived at his office and began compiling his quarterly report. The greenhouse's resource credit budget was finally balanced. Paul tapped the screen, beaming. This would demonstrate enough growth to keep investors confident in their viability. All he had to do was turn this into some of those very attractive charts the investors loved, and the greenhouse should be set for another year. Hopefully, he could assuage the investors enough to forestall the whole issue of drone harvesting.

Paul pinned a productivity report to the cork board, accidentally knocking down a few yellowed receipts. He stopped, smiling at the old postcards he'd forgotten were buried beneath data sheets and resource budgets. He pulled one down, a picture of a waterfall somewhere. Then he dropped it on his desk, pinned his report to the board, and moved on with his work.

IT WAS rare for Paul to take an extended break from his work, but the occasion called for it. Paul's eyes pinched in a grin as he waved at the toddler on the screen. The child lifted a tool from his mother's workbench, and Paul cheered.

"Oh, he's strong!" Paul cooed. "Come on Karl, buddy, let me see those muscles."

"Sorry Dad, we've got to run." The screen shifted and the toddler's mother appeared. "Karl has music lessons across town and our ferry leaves in ten."

Paul stuck out his lower lip. "Okay, Diligence. Have him call me after."

"Gardening club after, Dad. Then we'll be at the co-op all afternoon, and he's got that guided breathing class before bedtime. But we'll see you at the market in a few days. You got everything you need until then?"

Paul indicated that he did. His daughter blew a quick kiss and logged off. Paul stared at a blank screen where his grandson's face had been. At least the child was staying busy. Idle hands, and all that.

Paul groaned as he stood, rubbing his knees. Another badge of honor— a pair, in fact. He'd see his daughter and grandson this weekend, which was nice, but that also meant seeing the algae growers.

Another part of life, another necessary pain. Until then, he had work to do.

PAUL'S FINGERS TWITCHED. He felt like he should be doing something more productive than sitting on a bench under a tree. At least he was here with Karl.

"Grampa, wassat?"

Paul looked down at the 3-year-old tugging on his shirt, then followed the outstretched finger across the market. He felt his shoulders stiffen. "One of the Meanderthals' algae tanks. Your mom has work to do with them."

Paul noticed the children of the algae growers chasing each other around the market, jumping in puddles leftover from the rain last night. He looked down at his grandson and smiled. The child was engaged in a biogenetic simulator — much more educational.

The boy's mother kept busy too, although Paul wasn't always sure about the nature of her research. Diligence's lab had already produced new theories on energy-efficient desalinization, compost heat transfer, and hydroponic cycling. But lately, she had become fixated on a new project, something involving the city's algae-based bioreactors and microplastic decomposition. Paul's eyes narrowed, shifting from his grandson building hydrocarbon chains, to his daughter laughing with the algae growers.

It wasn't that Paul disliked the Meanderthals, per se. Nobody bred algae like they did. From the city's air filtration towers, to the nighttime bioluminescence that lit the streets, to the many algae supplements in their diet, the algae growers were vital.

But they were lazy. Paul hmphed to himself. Nomadic algae growers that used microbots and drones to do so much of the labor. They were transient, unaccountable. A band arrived, did repairs on public and private algae tanks throughout the city, and kept moving. They ambled from place to place, never in the same order, never with any sense of routine. Some people said they wandered just to wander, that it didn't actually benefit their work at all.

There was a reason people called them Meanderthals. It wasn't meant as a compliment, although the Meanderthals themselves had adopted the moniker. Paul hmmphed again.

Diligence waved farewell to the Meanderthals, and jaunted over. Paul stood up. Time to get back to work.

"Dad, I need a favor." Diligence said. Paul sat down.

His mind was reeling by the time she finished talking, but of course he said yes. It would be an incredible opportunity for her career. He could stomach a few days off from work, even if the thought made him sick.

But going to the Meanderthal camp? Staying overnight so Diligence could run tests on their algae tanks?

Paul gritted his teeth. If it had been for anybody but his daughter . . .

THE JOURNEY out of town was tense, at least from Paul's perspective. As for Diligence, she pointed out interesting plants along the road, bubbling on about her work with the Meanderthals. She tried to engage Karl in a nonsensical nursery rhyme, but the child was too absorbed in his simulator. Diligence went back to talking about plants. Paul sighed and watched the city shrink into the distance behind them. They'd better not try and implement drone harvesting while he was away. That would be just his luck. First personal day he'd taken in years, and he gets replaced by a machine.

Soon enough, the Meanderthal village came into view. Meanderthal pods listed to and fro, attaching or detaching themselves to the massive base unit, the village commons. The broad platform hovered over the hills, grasses churning below its suspension coils. Paul had seen large-scale magnetic levitation throughout the city — his own greenhouse used maglev carts for deliveries — but this was something else entirely. It was almost impressive. Shame it was being used by a bunch of transient Meanderthals who barely worked a day in their lives.

Diligence pulled their hovercar onto the platform. Watching out the window, Paul glumly observed the disordered array of Meanderthal pods dispersed across the untidy fields of the village commons. Children dashed between family pods and jumped over rocks, largely unsupervised. The adults were just as bad. They chased each other childishly, or lounged about playing instruments. Their algae tanks sat unattended, little bots stirring in nutrients or checking chemical levels. Paul glanced at Karl in the back and wondered how Diligence could expose her son to such terrible influences.

In the end, Paul kept his mouth shut out of respect for his daughter. She was here to do a job, after all. She powered down the hovercar and began the sequence to expand it into a temporary camper. She spoke to a few Meanderthals and embraced them warmly.

"Don't our hosts need to show us to our campsite?" Paul objected. One of the Meanderthals next to Diligence, introduced as Mark, laughed.

"There's no assigned parking," Mark said.

Paul was seriously weighing a plan to just hide out in the camper with Karl when a few Meanderthal children flitted over, chattering like squirrels, and whisked Karl away. Paul tried to protest, but Diligence waved it off.

He narrowed his eyes but said nothing, and began to unpack his bags. As if by magic he was surrounded by Meanderthals genuflecting before him, snatching his bags with choruses of "please allow me" and "I insist, sir."

Paul was ushered away and dropped into a folding chair someone placed for him. He huffed, ears burning. Did he look weak to them, or cowardly? Did he look like someone who couldn't handle the simple work of setting up his own camper? Paul felt a growl curling in his throat and was preparing to let these youngsters learn firsthand how capable he was, when he was interrupted by a chorus of snapping folding chairs and grunts from the five people who plopped into them.

"Heck of a nice day," the man next to Paul said, and the others voiced their agreement. "What's your name, friend?"

"Paul LaFalgue," Paul answered.

"Benito."

"Frank."

"Gloria."

"Ming."

"Norm."

"The only norm you follow is a glass of wine every night."

"I need it to sit through any of your stories, you rambling old fool."

The group traded insults back and forth, laughing raucously. Paul clutched the arms of his folding chair. All five were roughly his own age, and to see grown adults behaving in such a way chilled him to his core. There was no concern for the work of setting up the camper, or concern for their labor which surely needed tending to, or really any concern of any kind. The teasing melted into idle gossip, and Paul's attention drifted, wondering how his greenhouse was faring without him. He looked for Karl, and found him huddled near the group of Meanderthal children. Paul wondered if there was a polite way to excuse himself and go rescue Karl.

"But Sandhee's always been a rationalist. That's why he glosses over Wirthe's critique," Benito said.

Paul's attention snapped back to the conversation.

"I'm sorry, did you say Sandhee? Rakesh Sandhee?"

Benito asked Paul if he was familiar. Paul nodded. Sandhee's history of decentralized resource management was the talk of the city. But when pressed, Paul had to sheepishly admit that he hadn't read it yet. It was on his shelf, waiting. In fact, he didn't know anybody who had actually finished the thing. It was only published a month ago, and who has time for reading?

"Dad, can you grab Karl for his nap?" Diligence called, and Paul was only too happy to comply.

Once Karl was tucked into his cot, Paul asked Diligence about her progress.

"The community has been far more enthusiastic than I expected. They're letting me conduct my microplastic decomposition experiments in their personal algae tanks, but that means we'll have to stay longer than I thought," she answered.

"Three, four days tops. I promise. Then I'll get you back to the greenhouse."

She kissed him on the cheek and he felt a moment of genuine peace. Then, Mark the Meanderthal shouted that he had a question about some data sheet and she scooted off. Paul scowled.

LIFE over the next few days unfolded with a relentless lack of structure. Nobody owned an alarm clock, there was no standard time by which people began their work, and in fact it seemed that very little work was done at all. Paul watched Meanderthals tend to their algae gardens with loving hands, but only when the mood struck them. Otherwise, the Meanderthals . . . meandered. They popped in and out of each other's homes, gossiping, playing games of cards and dice. They wandered across their village commons, foraging for wild herbs and vegetables. Some left the village entirely, taking unscheduled holidays to go fishing or look at wildflowers.

Paul was uneasy, to say the least, and never quite knew what to do with himself. Every time he tried to be productive, some young Meanderthal would appear and insist that Paul enjoy the day and leave that chore to them. As soon as he sat down, the other old folks appeared, snapping open their chairs. Karl would be whisked away to play. Like Paul, Karl never looked fully comfortable, rocking on his feet as he watched the other children playing leapfrog or building little houses with sticks.

Then, one fateful day, Karl picked up a rock, and threw it at a puddle. It made a big splash and all the Meanderthal children were quickly upon him, laughing and cheering.

"Ever been?" Benito asked, and Paul realized that he had become so absorbed in watching Karl that he'd tuned out the conversation around him. Something about a rainforest somewhere.

"No, never had the pleasure," Paul answered. It didn't matter which rainforest Benito was talking about, because the answer would be the same. Paul had never been to that rainforest. Paul had never been anywhere.

"Shame. It's beautiful," Benito said. "Don't get out of the city much, do you?"

It was not an accusation, or said with any sense of judgment, but Paul still felt the words pierce him. He thought of the postcards lining his office, obscured behind reports and ledgers.

"Never had the time," Paul mumbled.

He turned from the conversation to watch Karl stack pebbles and sprinkle them with grass. A memory scratched the back of Paul's mind, and he saw another child, many, many, many years ago. A child who too jumped in puddles and scraped his knee on rocks and wandered aimlessly through golden fields. A child whose curiosity burned at the wide, marvelous world around him. Before that child spent a lifetime fighting the collapse of that world.

Unlike the Meanderthals.

Paul's own grandfather had been sure to pass that lesson down. When the apocalypse's footsteps could be heard just outside the door, there were those who worked hard to prepare. And there were those who left civilization behind, becoming nomads. Becoming Meanderthals. They lived lives of ease with their little huts and simple algae gardens, while people like Paul's grandfather fought against annihilation. And that labor did not allow for travel or holidays or jumping in puddles. But at least it had mattered. At least it gave him purpose.

Paul listened passively as the old Meanderthals traded stories of the many places they had been. Paul could envision the postcard for each destination. Karl jumped into the puddle alongside his rock and the other children squealed with delight. Paul sighed.

KARL'S INCREASED rapport with the Meanderthal children produced a mixture of contradictions within Paul. On one hand, he didn't want the laziness of the Meanderthals to rub off on his precious grandson. On the other, he couldn't deny the warmth he felt watching the boy giggle as he chased the others, his days unproductive and unstructured. It was confusing.

A much clearer issue to Paul was the problem of Mark. The most Meanderthal of them all, he awoke late and carelessly, rummaged around the fields of their commons for Lord-knows-what, and fiddled with the flute he was carving. And all before he started anything resembling work. Worst of all, from the moment they arrived Mark always seemed to be directly at Diligence's side.

Paul narrowed his eyes as he watched Diligence scurrying away. No, not scurrying. She was skipping. Like a schoolgirl.

"Sorry Dad," she said. "Just one more day." One more day to run those tests.

Their time among the Meanderthals had already been extended three "one more days."

Worried that Mark's unproductive attitude was interfering with his daughter's work, Paul feigned interest in the algae-grower and asked for a tour of the algae garden attached to his living pod. This will show Diligence, Paul thought. This will show her just how lazy the Meanderthal really is.

Mark did not disappoint. He showed up late to escort them to his pod and spent far too much time chatting with friends along the way. Paul chuckled to himself. Had he been an investor, he'd have already written Mark off as an unreliable worker, and an unserious person. In short, expendable. Exactly the sort of person to be replaced by a machine. Exactly the sort of person Paul was not.

Mark's algae garden was itself somewhat more impressive. Paul was surprised at the depth of knowledge Mark possessed about his algae, the breeding history, its biochemistry, recent research that was relevant, and so on. His stock was used for nutritional supplements, dried and powdered, and Mark was eager to provide samples for tasting. Paul was on the border of being mildly impressed when Mark ruined it all. Without any hesitation, Mark bragged about the drones that performed maintenance on the tanks, the programs that filed and filled orders from the towns they passed, and the bots that conducted vitality tests on the algae colonies.

Paul stared with horror at a man actively replacing his own labor. The only joy Paul got from the situation was the knowledge that he had succeeded in proving to his daughter that this Meanderthal was exactly the bumbling knuckle-dragger the name suggested. But when Paul looked at Diligence, the swell of victory deflated in his chest. She was positively beaming.

"Is Mark's algae going to be useful for your experiments?" Paul asked Diligence later. She shook her head.

"Not the type of algae I'm researching, Dad. Mark has been a big help though. He knows everything about every strain of algae bred here. I think he's taken a liking to you as well. And Karl."

Paul's ears twitched. He knew that tone in her voice. That was the same tone she used as a teenager when she was trying to convince him to let her see a late movie with friends, or ask for time off from the greenhouse.

Paul cleared his throat. "Mark's been spending time with Karl?"

Diligence shrugged. Still no eye contact. "You know what it's like here. Hard not to bump into everyone at least once a day."

Paul nodded. "Not like they're busy enough to do much but bump into each other."

Diligence mmm-hmm'd softly and scanned through her data. Paul's throat tickled with things he wanted to say.

"Just be careful," the words spilled out. "Mark's nice enough, as Meanderthals go, but not a good influence for Karl."

Diligence nodded.

"Because Karl needs structure," Paul pressed. "He needs to see the value of hard work."

"For what that's worth."

"What?"

Diligence set down her data. She looked Paul in the eyes.

"Every day at the greenhouse was a day you could have spent with Karl. You get that, right?"

"The sacrifices we make," Paul sighed. "If I'd ever let the investors think the greenhouse could demonstrate growth without me, they'd have sent me to pasture and automated my work long ago."

"So what?" Diligence said, venom on her tongue. Paul recoiled as if she had slapped him in the face.

"So . . . so what? So what if my life work is taken from me, given to some robot? Not while I still have strength to work, Diligence. That is not how I raised you! That time I spend working is valuable, my contribution to my society!"

"And did it ever occur to you how much I could have used your help?" Diligence spat the words out. "Ever since Scott died I've been doing this all on my own. I'm trying my best to raise Karl and do my research and work hard like you taught me but it's too much, Dad. It's too much. You could have retired ages ago with a full buyout, but you were always too stubborn, too determined to work all the way to your deathbed to even consider that I might need you! I needed you, Dad."

Diligence paused, shoulders trembling. Her face looked suddenly very much older than Paul remembered it.

"I'm just . . . tired," she said again. "You head on back to the city, Dad. Go back to the greenhouse. Mark can help me with Karl." Then she turned and walked away, leaving Paul as shaky, wordless, and white as a solitary ghost.

THE OFFICE FELT . . . quiet. It was not a peaceful quiet, not the comforting warmth that silence can sometimes offer, but a quiet that echoed, hollow, off the walls. It was a quiet that made itself known.

Paul stared at the work that had piled up in his absence. And stare is all he did. In an entirely new experience for him, he simply could not focus on his work.

Focus, Paul, he thought. Green thumbs do not grow on idle hands.

But when he tried to reach for his papers, his arms felt heavy. Just then, there was a knock at his door.

"Diligence?" Paul said, heart leaping into his throat.

"Afraid not," Benito smiled as he stepped inside. Paul's heart sank, and yet a sliver of joy remained. He offered Benito a seat, and a cup of coffee.

"What are you doing here?" Paul asked. "Do you have business in the city?"

Benito patted him on the shoulder. "I came to check on you, my friend."

Paul felt an unexpected rush of warmth, a tickle in his throat. He thanked Benito for his kindness, and the two talked. Paul told Benito what had happened with Diligence. Benito detailed years of conflict with his own son, who lived in a different Meanderthal village with his own children. They took the time to work through their issues, Benito said.

Paul offered Benito a tour of the vertical greenhouse, pushing through a thick canopy of green to show the Meanderthal around the hydroponic tanks, the gravity-drip features that reduced water waste, the lattices and trusses. Benito was an enthusiastic guest, asking questions along the way. But just as Paul felt he had made a true impression, he bragged that he'd stopped the investors from implementing harvesting drones. Benito tilted his head and asked why.

Paul opened his mouth to reply, when Diligence's face flashed in his mind. Benito took advantage of the pause.

"You have worked hard, my friend. Surely there is no shame in turning over some of the labor. I have used drones and bots my entire life, and my algae remains healthy."

"But think of how much more you could have produced if you'd worked alongside those bots, instead of letting them replace you," Paul sputtered. "You could diversify, attract investors, grow."

"I've grown enough," Benito patted his round belly. "My algae garden is like my belt. Any more growth and I'll be straining to keep it all together. I'm sure you know what uncontrolled algae growth means to an ecosystem. Devastation. You fear machines replacing you because you could work with them to produce more. But machines only offer salvation when they free us from work."

"Green thumbs do not grow on idle hands," Paul countered.

Benito rubbed his chin. "Never understood that one. Our algae thrive best in quiet waters. In fact, most green things prefer stillness. There are limits to how much, and how fast, anything can grow. Long before humanity wrecked the world, we knew this. We pruned and trimmed and burned and kept overgrowth at bay. Our cities forgot this."

Paul felt his ears burn. "Our cities had to endure the work of rebuilding the world after it collapsed. My grandfather helped build that world."

"As did mine," Benito nodded. "I remember how hard his generation worked to become nomads, to adapt. It was a difficult transition, full of challenges. Nomadism may have let them escape the fires and floods, but my grandfather fled so that one day I might wander. He worked hard so that I might know leisure. Is that not what we all want for our grandchildren? Better lives? Otherwise, what are we laboring for?"

The conversation continued on like this for a while, but eventually the time came for Benito to leave. Paul walked him to the front door of the greenhouse, and thanked him for the visit.

As Benito left, Paul turned to go back inside, but something had changed. His greenhouse had always been full, but suddenly it seemed more a snarl of jungle than a garden. Paul pushed his way through the leaves and greenery. The more he pushed, the more they seemed to try and grab him, restrain him, hold him back.

Panting, Paul burst into his office and shut the door. He took a deep breath.

Get ahold of yourself, Paul, he thought, and wiped the sweat from his brow.

Maybe just one or two drones wouldn't be so bad, just to help with the pruning and harvesting. Maybe . . .

Paul reached for a stack of receipts, but his hand grazed a postcard lying on his desk. He picked it up, looked at the waterfall.

In his mind, he heard his own grandfather, tired from work, still finding energy to tell Paul about all the wonderful places in the world. Visit them for me, his grandfather would say, once we've made a world that you can travel safely. Oh, the hours spent discussing the places they would go, the things they would see. Before Paul, like his grandfather, threw himself into the work of rebuilding that world.

Paul showed these same postcards to Diligence, these same wonderful places. And she too threw herself into her work without seeing one of them.

Paul set down the postcard and picked up the framed photo on his desk. He smiled at the picture of Karl, then sat down. There was work he needed to do.

It was two weeks later when investors entered the office.

"Stubborn old man finally agreed to mechanize some of the processes here?" One of them asked.

The new director of the greenhouse nodded. "All of them, in fact. We're ready to automate."

"And where is Paul?" another investor asked.

The director shrugged. "He retired. I think he took his daughter and grandson to some waterfall, somewhere. I heard something about them hitching a ride with the Meanderthals. I know his daughter was conducting research with them."

"So old Paul became a Meanderthal," the first investor chuckled. "How the mighty have fallen. Never thought Paul LaFalgue of all people would abandon civilization."

The investors laughed, then began sorting through the paperwork in Paul's office. They pinned receipts and reports to the cork board above his desk, not noticing all the empty pinholes there, never knowing those pins once held postcards from across the world, never imagining that those postcards were the only things Paul took from his office when he left.

ABOUT CHRISTOPHER R. MUSCATO

Christopher R. Muscato is a Pushcart-nominated writer from Colorado, USA. He is the former writer-in-residence of the High Plains Library District, a winner of the XR Wordsmith Solarpunk Storytelling Showcase, and a graduate of the Terra.do climate activism fellowship. He can very often be found not working. Follow him on Bluesky at chrisrmuscato.b-sky.social

Marginalia

Amanda M. Blake

At the boom that rocks through the compound like close thunder, Audrey blinks off the stream.

She already completed her morning education — flickers of mathematical equations, physics problems, stoichiometry, common chemical coding, and sentence diagramming beamed in and retained through breakfast smoothie additives for comprehension, memory, and focus. The streaming glasses block out all distractions; the additives block out all desire for them.

Once finished with school, she sank back and switched to entertainment, drinking in the images with peppermint tea and supplemental biscuits.

She is rarely interrupted during either stream; she is rarely interrupted at all. Unlike the more chaotic nurseries, this compound was built for those without children. Necessities are delivered on a schedule, extras on demand, but even for the young emancipated from family homes for purposes of tranquility, independence, isolation, and concentration, little more is required than the deliveries, a replicator refrigerator, and the bed and couch complimentary in a compound apartment.

Streams fill all other voids — comfort, stimulation, regurgitation, annihilation, the expiation of counterproductive impulses into calm equilibrium, enhanced and encouraged by supplements.

When she removes her glasses, the clean white and gray of her apartment appears unchanged and undisturbed. Under the streams, it can be difficult to tell what is dream and not. In the end, it's all one hallucination to another, strung together seamlessly, if senselessly.

The apartment lacks the richness of rooms through which the streams carry her, the context of possessions that no one needs to possess anymore, although some have them delivered, or reproduced if they have the code. It doesn't provide much joy, though, when they float through most of their waking hours. Audrey owns a vase; sometimes she conjures a flower. She has pictures on the wall, splashes of color that burst in her cortex like fruit soda bubbles. Otherwise, her world lacks texture, dust, even scent once she scrapes the remnants of meals into the disposal.

Sometimes, however, the outside world — abandoned though it is but for the barest of back and forth — intrudes in a moment of heart-skipping disruption. Like a substantial branch of the courtyard tree breaking under the weight and frailty of age, which brings some of the compound denizens to their doors to stare at the abrupt amputation. Like that time she got food poisoning from a delivery, preceding an apology and a soothing sympathy lassi in her next order.

She sets her glasses on the sill. The light through the half-closed curtains burns bright behind the daily overcast, no deeper gray on the horizon to hint at an incoming storm. Storms are uncommon, but violent when they occur.

Another boom, bigger than the first, quakes the apartment

and jostles her off her couch legs. Weekly electrotherapy bracelets maintain tone, but control is a less-required skill.

Audrey undoes the lock on her front door and pulls it open. Others have left their apartments, but no one seems the wiser for the cause. For some, that it doesn't repeat is enough to send them back inside, but there's a quality to the air that keeps her staring up into the colorless sky.

An odor she can't place, like food char but more bitter. A sound she can't place, similar to but softer than the ubiquitous effect of birds taking flight that she recognizes from most streams, as though they're contractually bound to include it, along with the relic cacophony of congested traffic.

Her tongue weeps for biscuits, and her close-sighted eyes blur and strain, but she follows the balcony walkway to the stairs, surer in step on every landing down to the tree's upended roots. She rounds the circumference of the compound's exterior, the same white stucco as the interior. Only on the other side of the compound are the distant plumes of black smoke visible, like trees rising in an impromptu forest. They crackle with tiny static sticks of lightning in the ion-charged air, encircled with tornadic debris of what looks like headless brown birds lifted by the thermals of heat before fluttering again into a free fall.

It would be safer to return to her apartment, but curiosity draws her away from the cylindrical compound to the street-boxed buildings of people glancing out their windows before closing them again, or peeking out the doors before retreating. Once the compound is out of sight, she isn't certain she can even make it back; she's never needed a sense of direction before.

The columns of smoke are easy to find, however, although she wrinkles her nose as the charry scent thickens and ash drifts down in a slow whisper of rain. The plumes rise and rise, spreading on the ceiling of the clouds and blending to spread temporary darkness, like what they call an eclipse in streams that recall a more varied sky.

Though out of breath and breathing bad air instead of what they pump through compound vents, she reaches the origin, an older rectangular building of pale brick rather than concrete. From its newly crumbled ruins spill boxes and piles of gutted, torched hardcovers.

Of course — a preservation site, a specialized cemetery of past-era miscellanea no longer required for anything other than reference, if not already replicated.

Preservationists maintain one of the last in-person occupations, as much forgotten relics as what they restore and conserve. The one who worked at this outmoded warehouse lays on the sidewalk in front of her building, her legs, hips, and abdomen somehow blackened dry yet pink wet at the same time. Audrey raises her hand halfway to her mouth. Death fills her streams, but it's never been real before.

This is not the only preservation warehouse that has suffered self-destruction. Tepid protests accuse the government of trying to trim fat from leeching grants or of eliminating any lingering traces of the past.

And maybe it's true, passively. Preservation buildings are all older, unconnected to services that nurseries and compounds enjoy, less regulated, less safe — not from people, who neither want nor need what the buildings contain, but from their own dated infrastructure. It's impossible for her to tell if this explosion is the product of sabotage or apathy.

With the ashes, wings of partial pages float to the hard ground, paving the streets and walks with strips of paper like burnt skin. Audrey tries to crouch down to inspect them, but she whimpers as her knees protest the pressure. She kneels instead.

These pages look neither like word streams nor the open books represented in entertainment. They're more like the blotted art in her apartment, shaped words surrounded by images and symbols. Stories have not disappeared; some still prefer word to image entertainment streams, although it has fallen out of favor among newer generations, who find its entertainment value too slow and soporific. When given a choice, Audrey streams stories she can see, but she's fascinated by the pages under her fingertips and frustrated by what has scorched away, lack of context in the scattered memories of an indeterminate past. Some of the words she understands. Some of the images she understands. She does not understand them both together; it's as though words were put to paper, then followed by piecemeal addition in the empty spaces.

She follows a flowering vine down the side of the page with the white shell of her fingernail as she studies the stylized script and searches for words, and within, their meaning.

"Ivy wound round to the top of the tower."

Audrey is startled by the echo of her own voice against the walls amid the low roar of the fire within the warehouse. She can't recall the last time she spoke rather than simply beamed her words into the digital sphere using an approximation of the sound of her thoughts. Her throat creaks from misuse, but it hasn't completely rusted shut, so she must speak sometimes, but like dreaming and streaming, it's sometimes hard to tell which side of the line she wakes on.

She glances about, afraid someone will censure her for disturbing the peace, but no one's there except the dead preservationist, reaching into the street, her wide sockets blank as though her glasses had embedded in her eyes. From her fingertips, though, scattered pages of hardcover castaways unsettle and scatter.

At first, Audrey thinks it's just wind through the tunnel of the gridded streets, but the dead woman's fingers twitch madly as dark green tendrils emerge from the nail beds, from cracks in the pavement, from the gutters. They twist with waxen leaves and bright pink petals, slithering over the streets and walks, over the brick of the burning warehouse and up the sides of nearby stucco-smeared buildings, finding rootholds in imperfections all the way to rooftops, where they stretch and bloom wide to a smoke-shaded sky.

Audrey falls back, and a pulse of the fire's heat rips the page away. In struggling to retrieve it, she rolls onto her belly to push herself up again and is instead entranced by the rough-written gloss jotted in the margin of the page beneath her hand. When her touch smears the soft marks, she jerks away, afraid she's ruined the relic, but it remains readable.

"the dichotomy of good and evil too simplistic, amalgam of both"

Another explosion from within the building knocks her into the tide of crawling vines and looseleaf pages. She gasps against the force pressing against her chest, shivers in the oppressive blast of heat that seems to cook the little hairs on her arms and brittle ends of her hair, but when Audrey raises her head from the protective cover of her arms, she doesn't smolder.

She reaches out like the body to gather the pages in, shielding them. The air she breathes low to the ground is better, but she swallows it in great gulps as though she's never breathed before, touches the pages as though she can feel ink in word and picture raised on the paper — stagnant yet somehow vivid, like her unpracticed speech.

She doesn't understand this new page, its words just short of legible, adjacent to familiar. She squints and turns her head for a new perspective. It doesn't help. The paper crinkles under her touch, thick but brittle with age. She's surprised it survived the fire and such a graceless landing.

Monsters grin and gambol down the margins. Her heartbeat quickens. Every second she thinks it cannot go any faster, it does, and doesn't stop. She wonders if she's dying, but she's never felt so alive as she does on the brink of her heart exploding like the preservation warehouse, leaving the ivy free to crawl over her like the other corpses in the street.

"Hic sunt dracones."

Audrey ducks, covering her head, at the deafening shriek from above, but she turns to the side, cheek against the inked page, as a creature erupts from one of the smoke columns. It rears three heads to the black ceiling of sky and spreads wings that span the block with a different kind of shadow. There is one monster, then two, three, four, each wheeling in a different direction and screaming flames of their own.

"This is real," she whispers. "This is me."

Audrey shudders like the edges of the pages around her as the monsters' howls rattle pipes and bones. Her ringing ears ache. Every joint and muscle protests her exertions and the bruising fallen upon tender, untested flesh. Her face flushes red from heat, from blood rushing through veins accustomed to a more languorous flow. She feels like the concrete beneath her pebbling into skittering gravel. As she tries to ground herself, she accidentally crumples an illustrated page with calligraphed text scrolled around soft curves and delicately-inked lithe limbs intertwined with a tangle of fabric and each other.

"Around them the moans and cries climbed until all were satisfied."

She bites her lip, shivering with something other than fear or cold. It has skittered at the edge of holographic experience, but never so strong, like falling out of bed without a floor. She swears lips brush her neck under her ear and that something presses broad and wet between her legs, something terribly, wonderfully physical instead of hallucination spells cast into her eyes through glasses.

With a whimper, she grasps the next page beneath, with a drawn finger pointing to different areas of text. Between columns detailing the adventure of a knight, a strangely random creature raises a scepter to genuflecting humans in the bottom margin.

"Rabbit?"

She yelps when a brownish-gray blur hops placidly into view near her shoulder. It takes a scorched page and chews on the corner with its nibbling little mouth. It regards her without fear, although it cocks its ears toward other sounds all around them — groans, wails, sobs, the moans and cries aforementioned, not streams but eddies, whorls, waterfalls, and rapids over the rooftops and through the streets, clashing in intersections.

Audrey climbs to her feet, clarity beyond dreams and streams in her vision and with awareness of each hair on her scalp, the movement of her toes in their slippers, the brush of her clothes on suddenly sensitized skin craving the fire's heat. Acrid smoke curls in her nose, but she doesn't try to wrinkle it closed.

She catches a partial page drifting on the awakened draft between the buildings before it falls onto her upturned face.

Vees of ink gloss the corners, with lilies in the frame of the incomplete text.

"Behold the fowl of the air."

Among the fluttering, flapping, floating pages, birds burst from blackest ink and screech to a sky that opens at last to vivid blue behind the still-billowing smoke.

A sound like their urgent wings rolls and twists from Audrey like the pages in the street, unfurls like the flowering vines — something she's heard through effects but never as powerful and unprecedented as the sensation that followed the tracing of fabric over writhing forms.

She laughs, joining her noise with the chaos symphony that breaks through monotony called peace.

She breathes, she sees, she seems, she seethes, she stretches to the black, crackling smoke and brilliant parting sky and reaches for the next page.

123

AMANDA M. BLAKE

A mass of tentacles and rose vines masquerading as a person, Amanda M. Blake is the author of such horror titles as QUESTION NOT MY SALT, DEEP DOWN, and OUT OF CURIOSITY AND HUNGER, dark poetry collection DEAD ENDS, and the Thorns fairy tale mash-up series. For more, visit amandamblake.com.

Unseen, Unknown

Mia Dalia

"Come on, come on."

I'm trying. I am trying. It just takes me a while. And my friend on the other side of the door usually knows better than to rush me. The knocking alone would have sufficed.

Now his voice throws me off, and I have to start over. All my patterns, one after another.

Finally, I step on a perfectly squared up and centered doormat and open up.

Xanny is all but hopping up and down with excitement. Or caffeine. Both tend to have the same effect on him.

"Look," he says and shoves his phone in my face. At least, he knows better than to shove it into my hands.

So, I look, but the image on the screen is nothing but a blur. I reach down for my reading glasses hanging from the loop between the second and third buttons of my shirt like they always do ever since I started needing them a couple of years ago. Magnified, the image comes into focus. Somewhat. Some of it is blurry in a way that has nothing to do with one's vision and everything to do with the photographer's limitations.

There are trees, lots of trees, and, if I squint just right, a largish shape in between.

"Are you seeing this?"

"I'm seeing . . . something."

"A Sasquatch. It's a freaking Sasquatch, dude."

Oh, boy. Here we go again.

I back up, so Xanny can come in. He pauses at the door, kicking off his slip-on sneakers — my friend is convinced laces are a waste of time — and bending down to put on the sanitary plastic booties from a box on the shoe rack. He is the only person who does this unprompted, and I appreciate it more than I say out loud.

Xanny and I have been friends for five years, seven months, and twenty-two days. It's a friendship borne out of fate and circumstances out of our control more so than shared interests and practiced commonalities. A few years ago, our mental breakdowns coincided, and we both ended up in Brookline State, a mental facility straight out of general casting.

There is one thing Xanny and I share: we both have OCD. It's different — mostly, he counts, and I clean, but it all stems from the same quirk of the brain. Our approach to managing it is different too. My friend takes Xanax, swears by it. I cope the old-fashioned way; the grin-and-bear-it way.

And yes, that is why he goes by Xanny. His real name is Paul. He hates it. The wrong number of letters; he hates everything to do with the number four, and Paulie just sounds stupid, so he went ahead and renamed himself after something he claims saved his life. And has his favorite number of letters. It makes sense to me.

Of the two of us, Xanny is the high-functioning one. He's smart enough and nerdy enough to have a full-time job in computers; one he can conveniently do remotely from his own apartment he can afford because he has a job. Me, I live at home, kind of; home-adjacent, I suppose is more accurate. It's all my part-time employment can stretch to cover. The arrangement is serviceable. I get a converted space above the family garage for nominal rent, my parents get the worry-easing closeness of their not-quite-master-of-the-universe kid. But it's far from ideal.

When Xanny isn't working, and sometimes even when he is, he's pursuing his true passion — cryptozoology.

I'd never even heard of such a thing until I met him. Now, I'm practically an expert just from being around it for so long.

My friend has never met a creature, real or imaginary, he wasn't interested in. He dreams of monsters. His walls are covered in posters and news clippings from every source imaginable. He combs the internet for sightings with regularity only someone with OCD can truly appreciate.

I don't really have anything like that in my life — an abiding passion like that — so I tag along with Xanny's.

"This photo was taken less than a week ago. And, get this, only three hours away from here. Isn't it awesome?"

He doesn't wait for me to answer as he's standing there with that goofy grin, practically bouncing on the balls of his feet. His keys jangle in the pocket of his hooded sweatshirt.

My friend looks like a Halloween skeleton someone took pity on and covered in skin. Most people on Xanax gain weight. If anything, he lost some, though going by the photos he's shown me over the years, he was always thin. The kind of thinness that makes his six-foot frame appear even taller. He's pale and has an unruly mop of black hair which makes him look like a character from a Tim Burton movie.

Also, he doesn't sleep much. He's addicted to Mexican Coca Cola, which he swears is better than the American version because of the real sugar used, and the way that combines with chemicals, natural and added, in his brain gives him a certain manic energy. I often struggle to keep up.

The no-sleep thing he compensates for by napping, though like most things he does, it's rather unusual. Not strategically spaced-out catnaps of Stanley Kubrick, not worked-all-day-tired dozing in front of the TV, not even food coma-induced passing out. Oh, no. Xanny drops off like a narcoleptic. Abrupt, spontaneous, random. It's something that takes some getting used to.

Right now, though, he appears fully keyed up. He taps his phone five times — the counting is still there, it's just less stressful for him — and repeats, "Sasquatch." The awe and wonder in his voice are palpable.

"You hungry?" I ask him.

He shrugs. "I could eat."

Despite his skeletal build, my friend does eat. A lot. But only when he remembers.

I make us both Cup Noodles. Arguably, Japan's greatest invention since Godzilla. Perfect food that's tasty *and* has the decency to come in its own disposable cup. Also, about as far as my culinary abilities stretch.

The above-garage apartment is essentially a studio, all one room with a corner for a tiny efficiency kitchen and a corner for a closet-sized bathroom. Space-wise, it's all I need. Privacy-wise, it's decent enough. The proximity to my parents, who insist my OCD is a "character quirk" and expect me to age out of it anytime as one might out of bedwetting, isn't optimal, but what are you gonna do?

For a stove I have a countertop two-burner which serves all my needs. I boil the water and pour it into noodle cups. Xanny, as always, gets the spicier one.

I pour water out of Brita into two red Solo cups and get two spoons out of a supersized container of plastic utensils. Et voila. A meal is served.

We sit at my small dinette set. Xanny takes the red chair, and I the blue. He's the only one that doesn't need the color coordination reminder, my most considerate guest.

My family, when they stop over, make the initial effort, but inevitably end up doing their own thing, resulting in hours of cleaning for me after they leave.

We slurp noodles at each other in companionable silence. My friend's phone is face up between us with the screen on, lest we forget his discovery.

Not that we ever would. Not that it's the first one, either.

Two summers ago, he was so convinced he found incontrovertible proof of the Jersey Devil that he dragged us all the way to the Garden State, where the legendary monster was eventually proved to be a particularly large and shaggy runaway Irish wolfhound.

That is not the sort of thing to stop Xanny. No way. My friend believes with a passion I can't help but admire in a world full of things unknown and unseen. He has this approach to life, this childhood wonder, that I've never shared, though often wished I could.

Back in the days of yore, when Earth was only partially known to its inhabitants, cartographers created maps where uncharted territories were marked with the legend 'Here Be Dragons.' Explorers of antiquity would set off to prove those legends wrong, to show that the world is nothing but land and water. Xanny would have traveled to find the dragons.

We finish the noodles, and I set two bananas on the table. I love bananas –nature's perfect fruit. Comes with its own holder and requires no washing or cutting up. I eat two of them a day. On special occasions, with peanut butter.

"So what are you reading right now?" Xanny asks. He's the only one who ever does.

I tell him about the latest novel. A story of a horror writer and his wife that spans nearly an entire century. The man gets obsessed with the occult and finding a way to be immortal, so he travels, and studies, and collects all these magical artifacts, which eventually end up at an estate sale. And every one of those articles wreaks havoc on the lives of people who buy them.

"Sounds interesting." My friend nods, though I know he prefers comics. They jive better with his attention span and jittery restlessness.

Back in the day, I might have shown him the book — it's got such a great cover — but I've been reading exclusively on Kindle ever since the device came out. It's really the best, most affordable, and, more importantly, cleanest, most OCD-friendly way to read. And I read a lot. More so lately. Kindle, for all its awesomeness, doesn't do covers justice, so I look them up on the internet. I'm a firm believer in cover appeal and judging the book by it. Say what you will, but it works.

Once we're done with our food, I clean up. Then noodle cups are rinsed out thoroughly and placed in a trash bin. The banana peels are folded and dropped into a small, lidded container. I don't compost as such, I just can't abide the fruit flies, which is what will happen if you put food scraps straight into the trash.

Xanny takes five small sips of water and launches into the tale of how he found the photo. It seemed to involve deep diving into highly specialized websites. I'm always impressed by how much of it is out there and glad Xanny can find people to share his interests, not just follow-alongs like me.

These people are all over the world, too. Everywhere there's an internet connection, there's someone who saw something out of this world and wanted to share.

I feel bad about serving water. I used to stock Mexicoke just for Xanny, but lately, my budget hasn't been stretching that far.

"So, when are you done tomorrow?"

I normally would be working tomorrow, at least a short

shift, but my hours got cut again. How do you fire someone for doing their job perfectly? You don't. You just slowly cut them down to nothing, whittle them away. That's my boss's strategy, anyway.

I don't mean to brag, but I do clean perfectly. You know that famous Schopenhauer quote, "Talent hits a target no one else can hit; genius hits a target no one else can see?" Well, I'm a genius at cleaning; I clean the dirt no one else can see.

Yes, it takes longer — I'm very thorough — but the results speak for themselves. Every surface is clean enough to eat off.

The thing is, people don't really want that kind of clean. They might say they do, but all they're really after is someone to get rid of the top surface dirt and dust, just so it looks clean.

Difficult to wrap my head around, plus, I've never been good with half-assing things. "Anything worth doing is worth doing well" is my motto. My grandmother, likely the smartest member of my family, used to say it. But no one seems to appreciate that approach.

"I'm free all day," I reply.

My friend gets it. I can see the sympathy in his eyes. "Oh dude, I'm sorry."

"It's fine." I shrug. "What are you gonna do?"

"I'll tell you what we're gonna do," Xanny says, his voice ramping up like a carnival barker. "We're going to go on a road trip."

OUT OF THE two of us, Xanny's the only one with a car. I bike or walk places. Public transportation is a nonstarter — too many variables. If circumstances force me, I can, in theory, bum a ride from my parents, but the messiness of their car, the bombardment of conversation, the yacht rock station their satellite radio is perpetually set to, is enough to make me want to jump out of a moving vehicle.

Riding with Xanny is much, much easier. For one thing, he lets me clean the car to my specifications before we go anywhere.

It's what I'm doing right now, Clorox wipes container in hand, while he's pacing around me excitedly.

He got here early and promptly dozed off in the red chair at the table while I was finishing getting ready. Now that I've premade our lunches (peanut butter and jelly sandwiches on wheat, two per plastic baggie, and bananas), made sure we have enough water, hand sanitizer, etc. I can work on the car in peace.

Xanny doesn't rush me, but I'm trying to be quick about it anyway. As quick as thoroughness allows.

The car is a white late model Honda. White is statistically the safest color on the road, closely followed by silver. I did my research before I went car shopping with Xanny. Subarus are statistically the safest vehicles, but Xanny went with Honda because the brand had five letters. This was my friend's first major purchase, and I wanted to help him make the absolute best choice. I think he did, all things considered.

I've never bought anything as big as a car. In fact, in all my adult life I have only once made a major purchase. It was recent enough to still sting. I had to sell a ring my grandmother left me. I know she probably was hoping I'd have someone special in my life to give it to, but it never worked out that way.

I've dated, sure, but the stress of it never proved to be worth it.

It's funny because sometimes I forget about my OCD or, rather, I forget to regard it as a disability. It's just a part of me, and so it's normal to me. But nothing, let me tell you, *nothing* will remind you quicker than other people. Their inability to see you, the person behind the glitches and twitches, is always, always, the sharp stick that pops your balloon.

In the end, I settled for a life of being unseen and unknown. I think that's why of all the esoteric cryptozoological creatures, I can relate to Sasquatches the best.

And then, Xanny came along.

Xanny sees me and knows me. It's a gratitude-shaped feeling too big for words.

Once I deem the car satisfactory, we set off on our journey. Xanny has programmed it into his phone, and a crisp, slightly metallic female voice is telling us what turns to take and where. We don't listen to music; we just talk.

You might think three hours is a long time to converse, but both of us are solitary creatures all too used to silence, so words build up, eager to spill out.

Each of us contains a world; the trick is finding someone to share it with.

The road disappears beneath our wheels at a steady pace. For the longest time, Xanny couldn't drive, but he had always liked it. Once the chemicals in his brain got balanced out properly, he came back to it with gusto.

It's stressful in the city, but out here, on the wide, open roads fenced in by an endless procession of trees, he's cruising like he was made for it.

I shift my sneakered feet along the now spotless footwell. I've been wearing the same style and brand for years until my final pair fell apart. For my last birthday, Xanny must have combed the internet to find the one remaining pair in my size. If I was given to strong emotions, I might have cried. Instead, I vowed to keep them pristine forever. I wear the beat-up old pair with super-glued soles to work. So far so good.

Xanny forgets his birthdays the same way he forgets to eat, but he has never forgotten mine.

My parents remember too. They give me fat cakes from the local bakery, one where the product sits sweating all day, inadequately glassed-in from the public. I usually try to force myself to eat a slice for their sake, then take it to my small apartment and dispose of it.

Xanny and I never run out of things to talk about. He combs the internet incessantly for the latest in the news of weird, and it makes me imagine a much more interesting world than the one I've always been stuck in.

Cryptids, aliens, monsters. Conspiracy theories. He separates the wheat from the chaff. Redacted government documents related to UFOs from the *Ancient Aliens* TV series. Although the latter is objectively one of the greatest inadvertent comedies on television.

I tend to stay away from the internet; it overwhelms me and pulls me under like the waves did in the one family ocean trip I remember clearly. The sheer boundless amount of information makes my OCD spin out in the most unpleasant ways.

The few times I do log in, I usually have a very specific mission in mind, a precise thing to find, or a particular acquisition to make. Afterward, I always feel drained, tired. Sometimes dirty too.

I do have a computer, but it often sits unused.

Xanny has three, and they are never off. My friend lives much more voraciously than I do.

As we drive, the city fades into a neat postcard image behind us, and then a steady procession of small towns dwindles until we can well and truly claim to be in the middle of nowhere.

It's desolate but also quiet, beautifully quiet.

"Could you live out here?" I ask.

Xanny weighs the question. "Technically, I guess. I mean, I can work and do research from anywhere. But I don't know . . . it just seems like—" He waves one hand nebulously for a moment before replacing it on the steering wheel "—a different world. *Their* world."

I wonder if he means the people who chose to live here or Sasquatches.

"It is peaceful."

"It is."

"And quiet."

"And cheap probably, too. I bet I could buy an entire house here."

For a moment, I let myself get lost in a fantasy of moving out here, living on Xanny's property. Maybe even *in* the main house. I never had a roommate. Living at home was traumatic enough. But who knows . . .

I brush the cobwebs of the daydream away.

"There it is," Xanny whispers, reverence in his voice, as the woods we've been driving to reach finally come into view.

The parking lot is stylistically surrounded by giant boulders. The woods, Xanny has told me, used to be home to several popular hiking trails, but lately, the cuts to the parks and rec budget have rendered those unsafe.

"We'll be safe, though," he assures me. "That's all just bureaucracy."

He gets out to stretch his legs; I follow.

"You ready to do this?" Xanny says, infinitely more energetic than me.

I sit down to put on a pair of modified hiking gaiters that will protect my sneakers. I was going to wear the old ones, but Xanny vetoed them, saying they had no traction left and I'd be slipping and sliding all over the place. Rolling on the forest floor categorically does not appeal to me, so I came up with an alternative.

"Do you want to eat now or later?" I ask.

He waves the offer off. Practical considerations are moot when excitement awaits. "Later."

We set off. The website where Xanny found the original photo offered approximate coordinates, the rest is down to the intrepid travelers and their spotty GPS navigation. Although Xanny also brought a compass, a map, markers (colorful ribbons to tie around tree branches) so we don't walk in circles, binoculars, and even a flare gun.

As a child Xanny was kicked out of boy scouts — the counting thing did not go over well with the rugged outdoorsy thing — but he does believe in preparedness.

We ascend a gradual slope that feels increasingly mountainous, the leaves or mulch or whatever it is are crunching under our feet. Nature is dirty, there are no two ways about it. I foresee a very long shower and a laundry load in my near future. There's no one I'd venture out like this for but my friend.

Once we complete our ascent, there's a flat clearing, like an observatory platform. With a pair of wooden tables and benches. The view is stunning. You don't even have to be a nature person to appreciate it.

"Now what?"

"Now we wait." Xanny grins. He's scanning the woods with his binoculars, eyes eager to spot something out of the ordinary.

I unpack our lunches, make sure he eats.

If there is a better sandwich combination than PB and J, I'm yet to find it. The trick is to use all-natural smooth unsalted peanut butter and a good i.e. fancy strawberry jelly. It's one of the few things I'll pay extra for. You gotta have some standards.

I don't know if Xanny tastes the difference; not the way he wolves the food down. Like it's keeping him from more important things. But he thanks me all the same and immediately goes back to his binoculars.

Early in our friendship, when we were both still tentative, still finding our footing, he told me about his obsessions, and I didn't know what to say. So I asked him why, why these things matter so much to him, and he told me that without mystery the world is too sad to bear.

Now *that* I could understand. My world has been sad for so long.

"And if you never find any of them?" I asked them.

"Then I will have had the pleasure of looking," he replied.

"And if you do? Will you tell the world?"

He considered it for a moment, messing with his already unruly mop of hair. "I don't really care about that," he said, finally. "I just want to see, with my own eyes, you know?"

I nodded.

A month later, for Christmas, Xanny gave me a clumsily wrapped box with five coconut-scented cleaning wipes containers. I love the coconut smell but because I go through so many cleaning products, I tend to stick with the cheaper lemon kind.

So yeah, that's a friend I'd endure hiking for.

It's difficult to understand why people do this recreationally. It's exercise, sure, all walking is, technically, but it's so uncomfortable. Compared to city walking, it's positively unwieldy. Is discomfort the point?

Is that why 'take a hike' has a negative connotation?

Outside of the view, I cannot recommend it. But then again, we're not here for me.

"See anything?"

"Trees," my friend replies, "lots of trees."

"What time is it?"

"Nearly noon, plenty of daylight left."

"Right, yeah."

Xanny would have probably stayed here all weekend, likely awake, just waiting and watching, but an overnight trip for me, even one featuring some local motel, is a different proposition altogether, and we both know it.

I take the second pair of binoculars Xanny brought for me and start scanning the woods.

We chat amicably about — what else — Sasquatch-related things. All the famous fakes, all the unconfirmed sightings, all the wild theories.

If the big guys *are* living in these woods, their ears must be burning.

A few hours pass. The weather is holding up, mild enough for a thin jacket over a sweatshirt, and sunny.

Xanny sprays us with five squirts of sunscreen each, and we vigorously rub it in. I'm surprised he remembered.

Nature isn't all that exciting after a while. It's like someone hit a pause button on a picturesque scene in a movie. Eventually, your mind starts spinning to the 'okay, enough, what's next' scenario. Well, mine does, anyway.

I check the time. It's nearly five. Which gets me thinking about how late we're going to be getting home and how much all my evening routines will be thrown off.

I look over at my friend. He's doing that pacing-bouncing thing, which I've come to know as his impatience dance. I don't want him to lose hope. Not everyone can hope as brightly as Xanny.

Just when I'm about to offer more sandwiches, my friend lets out a scream/gasp yelp that sounds like excitement damped down by awe.

"What? What?" I jump down from the picnic table I have been sitting on.

"The . . . it's . . ." Xanny for once is speechless. "Look," he finally exhales, pointing in what I believe might be a north-western direction. "Just look."

I train my binoculars to meet his pointing finger: trees, trees, wait . . .

"What *is* that?"

There's something there. Something impossibly huge and shaggy.

"Is that a bear?"

"Dude," Xanny whispers, "it's *him*."

"It could be a bear," I go on playing the devil's advocate.

I always end up doing that. When Xanny dragged us to NJ to look for the Jersey Devil last year, I was technically the devil's devil's advocate. Something only I found amusing, but still . . .

"Look at that posture. The erect gait. It's not even a question . . ."

Xanny sounds like he might cry out of pure happiness.

The figure in the woods is much too far to walk or even run to, but we can do the next best thing. Photos.

We live in the most photographed era of all time. It's a miracle there are any mysteries left.

Then again, everyone is mostly taking selfies, missing the grand picture. It's like that famous social psychology experiment where everyone is always missing the gorilla in the background.

But right now, my friend is zooming in on the grand picture. Tapping into the mysteries of existence. Click, click, click, until it's over.

"He's gone," Xanny says quietly, crestfallen.

Picking his binoculars back up, he scans the woods, but there's nothing. The magic was short-lived, but then again, most good tricks are. The longer you stay with it, the more you see the seams and wires.

"But you saw him. We saw him, actually saw him. Or, you know, her."

"Yeah," Xanny says, and a smile that can only be described as beatific lights up his face like the sun. "We did."

I thought Xanny would want to stick around afterward, indefinitely, hungry for another sighting, but my friend seems peculiarly content. Perfectly content. Happy even, I think.

He's never been greedy, merely curious. Now, his curiosity satisfied, Xanny is pleased, delighted, blissed out.

He lies down on a picnic table, and scrolls through his pictures, shaking his head as if disbelieving his luck.

"Like magic," he whispers.

I quietly agree.

Xanny drops off into a nap and I sit there and continue looking at the trees. Thinking how much it was all worth it.

I continue thinking that after he wakes up, while we eat the rest of the sandwiches and start heading back. Even the ride home feels different somehow, the way conquering heroes must have felt upon returning from distant lands and epic quests.

It was worth selling my grandmother's ring. Worth all the time spent on the internet hiring a veritable giant of a man willing to wear a custom gorilla suit for a jaunt in the woods. Worth having his friend spoof a picture of him dressed up for a trial run and putting it on the internet forum where I knew Xanny would find it. So totally worth it.

My friend can't hold his grin back as he drives us back to the world he's been making better for me all this time, and that I now, returning the favor, have forever made more magical for him.

When he drops me off at home, we exchange a knowing look.

"Some road trip, huh?" My friend smiles.

"Some trip," I reply. "And oh, Xanny! Happy Birthday."

Deep in the woods, a large hairy creature shakes its head. Humans, in his opinion, have always been weird, but this, as they say, takes the cake. This is the second time he is seeing a human male dress its weak-looking hairless body in a costume of fur and walk around in the trees. Very strange. Is it . . . impersonation?

He had told his family about it, and they shook their heads at him like he was making it up. After all, how would anyone know of them? They are always so careful, so good at camouflage.

The large hairy creature, whose name is too complicated for a human tongue to twist around, lets out a guttural laugh. Even if no one believes him, it's still a funny thing to have seen. The world, he has long suspected, is full of strange unknown things. Maybe, he thinks, he should get out more. Even though those of his kind who do, tend to come back bewildered and disappointed. The woods are very nice, and it's home, but he wonders about the world that lies beyond.

ABOUT MIA DALIA

Mia Dalia is an internationally published, Crime Writers Association-nominated author of all things fantastic, thrilling, scary, and strange. Her short stories of horror, noir, science fiction, mystery, crime, humor, and more have been featured in a variety of anthologies, magazines, literary journals, online, and adapted for narrative podcasts.

Her short fiction has been voted top ten of Tales to Terrify 2023 and shortlisted for the CWA's Daggers Awards 2024.

She is the author of the novels *Estate Sale* (BIF) and *Haven* (CamCat Books), novellas *Tell Me a Story* & *Discordant* (Anuci Press), and *Arrokoth* (Spaceboy Books), and the collection *Smile So Red and Other Tales of Madness* (Anuci Press).

Her upcoming work will be featured by PS Publishing, Spaceboy Books, Absinthe Press, Earthling Publications, and more.

You may find Mia here:
https://daliaverse.wixsite.com/author
https://linktr.ee/daliaverse

To Walk Forward, To Walk Back

Parker M. O'Neill

Six months ago, there was nothing I wanted more than to meet my father.

My mother never had a Link; she died shortly after I was born. She's out of reach. Sealed away completely behind the veil of death in a way my father is not.

When I was too young to remember, he brought me to Fort Hill. He smuggled me through the AgCorp zone and ended up gut shot by Pinnacle drones. He dragged himself the rest of the way, living just long enough to get me here safely and name me Amaranth. Kateri and Francis — an elderly couple who'd always wanted a little girl — took me in and taught me how to be Onöndowa'ga:'. I always knew that one day I would meet him, though. Kariwase.

The Walk Back requires only two things: that you have a Link, and that one of your parents had a Link. My father installed mine at birth. But it's not until you reach twenty-four years old — adulthood, supposedly — that you can Walk Back; connect with your ancestors. Learn from their wisdom.

Their mistakes.

Our society is *built* on the Walk Back. The actions we take today will resonate down through seven generations — and what better way to learn the bitter pain of failure, the joy of success, and the quiet reward of a life well lived than to see across time?

I studied for months. I practiced. I was not born here; I was not born into the Onöndowa'ga:'. I *needed* to succeed.

I knew it wouldn't be easy. They told me my father had likely spent most of his life out of range of a Link tower. To Walk Back to him would be vague, fuzzy. Not like the others. Some of them had family lines running back four or five generations; back to the technology's invention. I couldn't imagine what it would be like to see so far back, but I craved it. It wasn't that I relished the challenge of my unique circumstances. But I so badly wanted to meet him.

I remember feeling the buzzing in my Link for the first time as I stepped into the stony garden of the Walkways. I moved forward, eager, eyes blurring as my vision doubled. For a moment the garden was shrinking, not a place anymore but the memory of a place, a distant dream — and then I was through. I was about to meet my father.

It was dark and cold and quiet. Odd that the first sensations I felt were negations — not the presence of something, but the absence of everything. Then I looked up — *he* looked up — into a sea of stars.

I felt small. My legs — *his* legs — moved mechanically under me — *us* — carrying us across a broad, dry plain. How long ago did this happen? We were hungry and cold and exhausted. Sandwiched between two flat expanses, the dry grass under us stretching in every direction unbroken and quiet, the starfield above wider even than the plain. I felt straps on our shoulders supporting a heavy pack on our back. Where were we going? I strained, listening, looking, feeling. An impotent passenger along for the ride. It was raining. Quietly and distantly, but it was raining. Why would my father remember this moment?

Our Link buzzed, pinged — a moment of warning before the vision blurred and changed — and we were in a kitchen. Mushrooms, onions; rich scents filled the air. We were stirring a pot on a stove. It was an action I had done a thousand times in my own life; with my own body, with my own Link recording memories for future generations. For just an instant I felt closer to him than I ever had. *This* was what the Walk Back was for. I could live with having only disjointed snapshots of him if it meant having something at all.

Then it changed again. We rushed forward in time, a split-second vision of Fort Hill — it must have been as he carried me there, dying — and then back again, reversing and racing through the years. A burst of sound and heat. He was in a forest, fire crackling all around. But it wasn't a wildfire. Screams, confusion. Branches snapping like chalk and great resounding blasts that left a void of quiet and peace for a millisecond before the screams redoubled. Our hands held something, a length of cold metal or heavy plastic. A weapon, even to my untrained eye. Something moved in the brush ahead of us, and I could feel our blood racing. Time slowed. A face resolved among the trees.

A face I recognized from a hundred Link posts. A leader to our people, and a martyr: Hasanoanda.

My father pulled the trigger.

THEY HAD to drag me out of the Walkways. I was insensate. Otetiani carried me home and my grandparents cared for me and cried with me. They hadn't known. They only met my father once, on the day he brought me here. The day he died.

Who could have known what kind of man he had been? Who could have known?

A COLD SPLASH AND A FROWN.

The signal I send to Otetiani is more of a feeling. Link messages *can* be words or pictures, but I like being able to say more with less. I turn in time to see her shivering at her table by the windows. Message received. She sends a feeling back — a warm breeze. Her way of saying *sorry, but it was for your own good.*

I'm busy for the rest of my shift, mostly working the prep counter in the back. There's lots of work to do — shucking corn, rinsing beans, roasting squash. Our traditional staples, mixed and remixed in a hundred ways over the centuries, given freely to anyone who needs food. Normally I'm happy here, even on days like today when patrons arrive not in trickles but in droves. But I'm stewing — a little annoyed at Otetiani, mostly dreading tonight.

Otetiani sticks around until the last few patrons head out, lounging in a chair like a mountain lion after a hunt. Just looking at the muscles of her arms makes me ache. How many days working in the fields did it take to look like that?

I drag out my closing duties; anything is better than going to the Walkways. And it does calm me down a little. I've never found anything that feels as good as feeding the hungry.

The sunset is already bleeding across the sky by the time we get moving. We head east to the Walkways through what some people still call downtown — new transplants, mostly. Fort Hill is a fraction of the size of the nearest dead city, it can hardly be called *downtown,* but we're the largest free settlement around.

The younger newcomers will get used to the slower pace of things. At least, I did.

"It was kind of a stab in the back, that's all," I say.

"At least I got Virgil out of your face," Otetiani says. She's always smiling, always sunny. "He wasn't going to leave you alone until he heard a 'Yes, Virgil, I'll see you at the Walkways tonight.'"

"Easy for you to say. The public Walk Backs are *boring*. You and the others get to learn your family history. I get to watch public access lectures on how to grow algae." I don't mention how even the thought of stepping into the Walkways makes me nauseous, but she knows anyway.

"So take my advice and study crop diversity this time. Do you know how different our fields are today compared to even just thirty years ago? They didn't have half the stuff we do. AgCorps owned most of the cultivars. It's actually really interesting." I roll my eyes, and she changes tactics. "Plus, it'll get everyone off your back for a while. And, I mean, it *is* important. You can't just skip it forever." She sends a pulse of warmth over Link, softening the words. The equivalent of a smile without having to turn and break stride. It helps, and she's right. But the Walk Back and Kariwase are inexorably tied, now. I have to do one and I hate the other.

"And I'll be there for you if anything goes wrong this time," she says, suddenly serious. Her brown eyes latch onto mine for a moment.

Then her joking demeanor is back. "Virgil will probably wise up soon. That one could use some wisdom from his family line. Chasing after a woman who's not even interested in—"

"That's far enough, thanks." She stops. But I'm smiling, and she knows I am. She pushes me when I need it — like forcing me to come to the Walkways, unfortunately — but she never goes too far. What would I do without a friend like her?

The sun's rays fade as we climb the hill. The streets below

our feet glow faintly, solar-powered bioluminesca softly bleaching the ground with pale light. Trees can be found anywhere in Fort Hill, but nowhere more than the crest of the hill, where the Walkways sit. I can feel my Link buzzing in anticipation, in anxiety. My grandparents used to take me here when I was young; we pretended we could see the shore of Lake Ontario. I know better, now. On a clear day you can just make out the silhouette of the dead city to the north, but no further.

There's not much ceremony once we're inside the garden. The Walk Back *is* the ceremony. My vision doubles as I stride between Link towers, boxwoods and lilac—

I Walk Back.

IT DOESN'T GO WELL.

I'M HALFWAY home before Otetiani catches up to me. I knew she would; I hoped she would.

"Ama, I'm sorry," she says, breathing hard.

"It's not your fault," I say. I can barely get the words out. I slow down, stop; we're standing on the side of the road. Lit by the moon and the glowing footpath with crickets for a chorus. I can't look at her. My cheeks are red, shame-tinted-with-anger. Why is it so much easier for everyone else? Why am I the only one who can't keep it together?

"I shouldn't have pushed you to come tonight. It's absolutely not your fault if it's still traumatic. I'm sorry I made you. Maybe we can ask for some kind of exception. I'm sure your grand-mother would understand—"

"No, it's . . . in the Walkways, I saw him."

"Your dad? You were using the public line, right? He couldn't be there — I mean, I don't understand how he could—"

"Not him. I saw Hasanoanda."

"Oh." She deflates. "Oh, shit, Ama, I'm sorry. What was he doing?"

It actually feels good to talk about it, so I tell her what happened. Tears come, and comfort follows in the form of her arm around my shoulders. It's unexpected, a bright spot on a gloomy canvas. The sun on an overcast day.

The public lines exist for two purposes: general education, and people like me. It's easier to learn while you're occupying the mind of a scholar equipped with a specialized Link. But for people like me, it's all we have. My grandparent Francis, for instance — their parents were newcomers, fleeing a dead city to the south. Their parents never had Links, had never even heard of the Walk Back before coming here, and so Francis has no ancestors to connect to. It's not as simple as installing a Link on a newcomer. It has to have been there since childhood, and regularly connected to a Link tower, or else you get—well, you get my father. Blurred snatches of memories.

I thought I'd be safe on a public line. I didn't think there would be anything to remind me of Kariwase. But apparently, Hasanoanda liked to visit the fields back then, forty years ago when the public line was recorded. Before we had our Three Sisters returned to us—corn, beans, squash. Hasanoanda was *hoyaneh*, an old Onöndowa'ga:' title. He was a kind of militia leader, a hero who kept the AgCorp Pinnacle from stealing our land and burning our fields. All our lives we've been told how he fought them off, how he beat back the last of them as he died. And six months ago I learned that my father killed him.

We're at a table at our favorite cafe, oak-shaded and quiet. The night is clear and breezy, and for once almost nobody else is around. Maybe everyone stretched their legs enough during the unusually nice weather today. The rainy season will be coming soon, with summer on its heels, during which it will be far too hot to move around much until dark. In a way, the damage done by our ancestors resulted in our vibrant nightlife. We can't undo it, but we can adapt.

I take a sip of my smoothie and ask Otetiani to tell me about how her Walk Back went. It's cold and sweet and lingers on my tongue. She smiles at me and I still my hand, resisting an impulse to wipe away the salt-streaks on my cheeks. The ghosts of tears, residual like the smoothie's sweetness.

She tells me she visited her grandmother's life today. The most important step in learning to Walk Back is practice, but other factors, even the weather, can have an influence on which ancestor you wind up visiting. Otetiani's grandmother always loved warm, faintly windy nights like tonight. With concentration, the similarity can be brandished like a key.

She worked in the fields too, in the tumultuous time of AgCorp attacks and seed droughts. The AgCorps back then were powerful and brutal. Hungry for the power they had once held. The cultivars they peddled were altered — gene-locked to produce no more than a single season of crops before dying.

"They were in the business of starvation," she says, "and control."

"Thanks. This is really cheering me up."

"Sorry." She shrugs, in person and over Link at once. "But look at how much we've reclaimed from them. Aren't you interested in learning where your food comes from? You're the best chef I know, but you never come out to the fields."

"Do I need to know more than the basic principles? Beans climb the cornstalk, the corn is stabilized by the beans, and the squash leaves keep the weeds away."

"I'm impressed," she says, sipping her smoothie, and she even has the grace to look like it. But there's a glint in her eye. "So do you think they'd grow just as well separately? Do you think they don't benefit from each other?"

"I see where you're going with this."

"We're the same way." I raise an eyebrow. "People, I mean," she says. "We need each other. And your father — shit, Ama, even if Kariwase was a dyed-in-the-wool Pinnacle drone, you're not him. You can heal from what it's done to you — you *have* to. And you don't have to shoulder this alone. You're not a — I don't know. A mushroom."

We look at each other for a moment before we both burst out laughing.

She blushes as we walk to our homes, alone on the street but together under the moonlit night.

ENNUI, and the feeling of an impatient tapping foot.

I'm standing outside Otetiani's apartment, watching the weather panels slowly shift from *shine* to *rain* as the droplets begin to fall. Another relic of the climate damage done in the past; it'll rain and storm more days than not from now until summer. But the weather panels draw kinetic energy from the falling drops, and the waves of Lake Ontario provide hydroelectric power.

I'm nervous. And not just because of the fact that we're going to talk to Hasanoanda's son, at Otetiani's behest. Something feels different. I'm not sure what it is.

She bursts out the door, still putting on a jacket. She smiles at me. I guess she got my message. I can't help but smile back.

Why is he so calm?

Eric is in his early 40s, wiry, with just the hint of his father's sharp features. Even that slight resemblance is like a gut punch. The two of them exchange pleasantries; I just nod along, my skin going clammy. I feel like a block of ice, a cold and numb thing on the verge of shattering.

Otetiani Links me a sense of warmth. Care. Letting me know she's here.

We're at a little communal garden on the west side of town, a canopy strung between saplings to shield us from the rain. Sitting among the hydrangea and ivy, Eric looks at peace. And then he finally addresses why we're here.

"I saw him, you know," he says slowly. "Your father. I was a teenager when he brought you here. He was bleeding from a dozen wounds and carrying you. What were you, two years old? He carried you like you were the most precious thing he'd ever held. Like all the weapons and bombs and AgCorps of the world couldn't hurt him, so long as he had you.

"Years later, I saw a younger man in the Walkways, in my own father's final moments. It wasn't until I heard what happened to you six months ago that I realized the two men I saw were one. I'm sorry, Amaranth."

I'm stunned out of my silence. He's apologizing to *me*?

"My father killed yours, Eric." The words come out in a rush, almost unbidden; they hang in the air like an oil stain. It's the first time I've said that out loud. I don't feel freed by having said it. I feel sick. "You don't have anything to apologize for."

"Neither do you," he says. "Amaranth, I hated the man who killed Hasanoanda. First when I had to grow up without ever knowing my father, and then later when I watched it happen through my father's eyes. I lost years to that hate. But I've made my peace with Kariwase."

Otetiani's hand on my arm is the only thing keeping me up. "How?" I manage.

"There were feasts and days of public mourning when Hasanoanda died. As I grew up, I learned about him from a hundred of his friends, a thousand Link posts. And still none of it was what I yearned for. I knew I would meet him myself someday, in the Walkways. So why should I take anyone else's word for what he was like?

"There's no shame in wanting to look backwards for wisdom and advice. I think the Walk Back is an amazing technology, and I think it helps us far more than it hurts. But you can't *just* look back. You can only make things better by looking forward."

"What are you saying? What does that have to do with her father?" Otetiani's voice cuts across the garden, fiercely protective.

"Look at the life he lived. We only know two things about him — that he killed my father, and that he brought you here. One act of evil, and one act of good. Twenty years separate those two acts, Amaranth. He lived a lifetime in that gap. I'm not asking you to forgive him. Only to try to understand who he was. The person that he was and the person he became. Do you think he didn't learn anything in all that time? Do you think he didn't change?"

"I . . . how should I know?" I'm breathless, whispering.

"Go and ask him."

Otetiani and I are walking back towards the center of Fort Hill, neither of us acknowledging that we're approaching the Walkways, when the rain intensifies. It comes down in sheets, lightning spearing down from the clouds overhead. We're taking an unfamiliar path—circuitous, rambling, just enough plausible ambulatory deniability to convince myself I'm not on my way to retraumatize myself in the Walkways. It hangs in the air between us, unspoken. Neither of us wants to break the spell.

And it's there on that unfamiliar road that I'm overwhelmed by déjà vu.

I double over; she's on me in a flash. "You alright?"

But I can't explain. Because it's not that I've seen this before—

It's that *he* has.

He carried me down this road, trailing blood and dragging his feet, in a rainstorm just as violent and raw and regenerative as this one. I'm certain of it, and in that instant I know something without ever being told.

My father loved the rain.

I break into a run, beelining for the Walkways. It's slick, and I'm running uphill, but I'm exhilarated. Driven. She's following, keeping pace easily, shouting apologies to the people we hurtle past.

I almost make it.

I'm not an athlete. I work in a kitchen. I go down on one knee, half-slipping and half just running out of steam. The Walkways taunt me, all weathered stone and Link towers in among the lilac, up there on the hill no more than a quarter-mile away and yet unreachable.

I close my eyes, panting, and suddenly the ground is falling away from me. Otetiani's sending me a calm blue peace over Link and—

Is she picking me up?

She shoots me a smile, eyeing the furious red on my cheeks. Neither of us speak; it's another thing unmentioned. Another spell unbroken. But I feel like a pumpkin.

She's strong and gentle and before I know it, we're on the hilltop. She puts me down at the entrance. "Go on," she says.

I hesitate—

And grab her hand. I want her with me. She won't be able to see my Walk Back, but I can't do this alone.

A forward step.

Link buzzing.

Double vision.

IT'S RAINING.

We're in the forest again, the place where he killed Hasanoanda. Is it . . . afterwards? There are burned bushes all around. Lilacs. We look up, following the droplets down from a cloudy sky to the scarred forest below.

He drops — no, *we* drop — the weapon. Adrenaline floods away, the moment over, and the draining sensation is replaced by a burning meteor in our gut.

We killed someone. Our thoughts, his and mine. But before I can get comfortable in this body and in this time and place, the world blurs.

A shift—

We're older. Mid 20s, maybe. It's raining here too, on the plain under the vast field of stars. There's a heavy pack on our back. Am I in it? The child-me? No. He's too young. We're heading east and the field around us is a wide expanse blanketed by the gentle hush of the falling rain. A blur, a rush, a lightning bolt—

Back. We're sixteen, running away from home. Heading west, out of the Kanien'kehá:ka lands, away from our father, going further and passing even Fort Hill to go where no one will ever find us — Pinnacle.

Forward. We're eighteen and full of anger, hating the world. Pinnacle doesn't give us purpose; it embitters us. This is the year we kill Hasanoanda, and I know it, but my father does not.

Forward again, almost two decades, and I'm looking at a face that's very like my own. She's in her 30s, thin, but she has my curls, my smile. My mother.

"She'll be able to see this?" she asks. There's a seriousness verging on sadness in her eyes. A slight curve in her belly, where her hands are resting.

"I'm not a Link tech. But I think so, someday."

She meets our eyes. "Then listen to me, Amaranth. I love you. Don't ever forget that." I *yearn*; I never thought we'd meet. She tears up and it feels like we're going to, too. I imagine a hand squeezing mine. "Don't be as hard on yourself as this one is." She scratches us on the chin; a laugh bubbles out.

And she's gone, or we're gone, rocketing back along the line and settling somewhere in our 20s. Twenty-four. We're twenty-four. If we were in Fort Hill, it would be time to learn our family history. But we're in a field, that same starry field, only finally reaching the edge of it. We walk for a time in quiet company. The strain in our legs is like an old companion, we've walked this path many times. Or — it's fuzzy. Suddenly, I'm certain that we *will* walk it many times.

His anxiety swirls and mixes with my own as we come to a place that we both recognize. So much of the forest burned away in that old battle. But there's new growth. Saplings, wild-flowers. A gentle arc of them surrounding the grave of a hero. There's a split-second step backwards — whispering *I'm sorry, I'm so sorry* to the man dying right here years before — and forward again, slowly sliding the heavy pack off of our back and setting it in front of the gravestone. The grave is well-kept, the flowers cultivated; someone will find it here sooner or later.

Tears cloud our vision as we unfold a sheet of algae-paper. I catch a glimpse as we set it down but my father already knows the words by heart and suddenly, I do, too.

I go cold as I hear them in my mind.

Tell your people that you ambushed a Pinnacle convoy or that you found these in a dead city. Don't tell them the truth. But send someone to check this place on today's date every year. I can only make so many excuses before Pinnacle figures me out.

This package contains two things that Pinnacle stole from you long ago. From everyone. I'm trying to give them back. The kernels and the beans in here are from Pinnacle's private fields — their intellectual property. Unlike the products they sell, whatever you can grow from these will give you seeds again and again. Next year, I'll bring squash of as many kinds as I can smuggle.

If nothing grows, I'll try again a year after that. And again, and again, until the Three Sisters are returned to you.
I once killed in Pinnacle's name to keep these seeds from spreading. I cannot pay off that debt, not ever, but I am so, so, sorry. I bring them now, freely; not to settle a debt but to make things better.

Plant them, grow them. Please. Make something new out of something old.

Thank you.

I OPEN my eyes in the garden, lying flat on my back. Pillowed by soft grasses. She's here with me; she's kneeling beside me. She's squeezing my hand with one of hers and running the other over my forehead, until she realizes I'm awake.

"How'd it go?" She sounds nervous. I probably look awful. But I feel — I'm not sure how, exactly, but different. Resolved.

There's a lot I need to process.

"I'm not sure I can forgive him," I say finally, "at least not yet. Even if everyone else already has. I had to watch him kill someone. He said it himself. He can't make amends. He can't change that."

She waits.

"But," I start. "That wasn't all he did. He lived a whole life, Otetiani; bad and good. You might even be interested to hear some of it." I send a little wisp of mystery over Link, and her face splits into a smile. A *lot* of people would be interested to hear how our Three Sisters came back to us. But is that story even mine to tell? "I don't know how to feel about him. I might not know for a while. But I know that he did bad things — unforgivable things — and then later, he did good things. He wanted to be better, to *get* better. To improve things for the generations to follow him. I want that too."

We bask there for a moment. The rain has stopped, but next time it comes, I'll be here again. I want to know more about him. I want to know as much as I can. I still feel that yearning, but there's something new where the hate was. Is it grudging acceptance?

Kariwase made terrible mistakes and he spent the rest of his life suffering for them. I don't want to be like him in that way. But I can learn from his mistakes. I can build something better for myself, for everyone, out of what he's given me.

Actually . . .

There is one mistake I've made. I hope it's not too late to correct it.

I hesitate a moment before throwing caution to the winds. Why not be impulsive twice in one day? Is my Link recording this? I feel delirious, but I forge on. "Thank you. For everything, Otetiani. I never would've done this without you. I never would've been *able* to do it without you." She smiles and starts to stand. I realize she's still holding onto my hand and I pull her back down, pull her just a little closer. Her eyes widen a fraction.

"You've always been here for me. You've supported me so much. You've been more than a friend to me. I can't believe I didn't see it earlier."

There's a split-second warning, a red rush over Link of pure, raw *emotion*.

Before she throws her arms around me — she's always been so good at knowing what I want, what I need — and our lips meet, and everything is beautiful there among the memories and lilacs.

ABOUT PARKER M. O'NEILL

Parker M. O'Neill writes from upstate New York, where he started his creative career with a fifth grade video of the family dogs. He hopes to someday surpass that artistic high. He is a recent winner of the Elegant Literature Award for New Writers, and his fiction can be found in Apex Magazine, Flame Tree Press, Crepuscular Magazine, and elsewhere. Find his socials and some of his other work at https://linktr.ee/parkermoneill.

Museum of Humanity

Camden Rose

$\mathcal{T}$he door creaked as I opened it, light cascading through the glass in a thousand tiny fragments that reminded me of my favorite show as a kid: *The Speed of Light.*

The opening credits showed three young adventurers running through a rainbow, as though etched into stained glass. It was my first introduction to Elise Montgomery, my favorite screenwriter. I lost myself in the show, choosing another episode over eating or sleeping.

Not that we had the pleasure of TV anymore. Not since people started dying, coughing and falling ill, only to sleep and never wake.

At least we didn't almost run out of oxygen like the kids in *The Speed of Light.* I could count on that resource outlasting humanity. Oxygen mattered in space and, despite my best attempts, I was still on the ground.

I closed the door with my foot while hoisting my sack over my shoulder. It was getting heavier with each house, and the burlap scratched into my skin.

There had to be something I could take. There was always something of value, and I'd become the expert at determining what each person held dear. Cookbooks, family jewelry, a drawing by the kids of the house. Anything could work as long as it mattered to the people that had lived there.

I shifted my bag to my other shoulder, then remembered there was no one to steal it. I hadn't seen a person in weeks and, if anyone was alive, I doubted they'd take my stuff. I placed the bag on the tiled floor, balancing it carefully, so the contents wouldn't fall out. I sighed, grateful the rashes on my shoulders from the burlap got a much-needed break. I looked around the front room.

To the left, a hallway led to a kitchen. To the right, a set of stairs led up to what I could only imagine to be bedrooms. Right next to me, a side table sat piled high with coats. I walked to the kitchen quietly, afraid to disturb the dust coating the appliances. Most people didn't keep their most valued possessions in the kitchen, but every now and then I'd stumble upon an old family cookbook or recipe — the generational treasures, the true essence of humanity.

Money meant nothing now, but memories were priceless.

The first cabinet had nothing but spices and moldy bread. I closed it and moved on to the next one when someone upstairs coughed.

I paused, my hand hovering over the sink like an astronaut immobilized by takeoff.

Most houses were empty. I hadn't seen another human — alive, anyway — in weeks.

I thought everyone died but me.

"Hello?" I called. My heart beat over my eardrums, silencing my senses.

I took a deep breath, trusting that my immune system would continue to protect me. My desire for any human connection overpowered the logical response to flee. The floor creaked under each step I took on the way upstairs.

The first door upstairs opened to a kid's room, furnished with a small bed and space-themed accessories. From the galaxy comforter to the toy spaceships floating from the ceiling, I found my childhood desires returning to me. If only my parents could have afforded such luxuries. I'd had to chase my space dreams all on my own. And now they were dead, one gone before the pandemic and one during. I closed the door and moved on.

The next room juxtaposed the rest of the house. Chaotic and messy, it smelled of old paper. The walls were covered in sticky notes and bookcases. A leather chair sat in the middle of the room, but papers piled high on the cushion, so I doubted whoever lived here ever actually sat in it.

To the left, nearly covered in sticky notes, hung a framed movie poster that looked familiar. I had only seen online versions, so my hunch might have been wrong, but I'd bet it wasn't. I pulled off a sticky note labeled, *"Space is vast but people are small."* Then another that said, *"What if she didn't make it?"* in almost illegible handwriting. I peeled off more, feeling like an adventurer uncovering treasure. Slowly, the image revealed itself, making me gasp in awe and forget briefly about the person who had coughed.

In the poster, a woman in a spacesuit floated in front of one of the moon's craters, darkness all around her. Above her, in typed cursive, lay the title: *Luna and the Moon.*

That movie inspired me to become an astronaut myself. I wanted to reach the stars like her. I completed the training and was preparing for my first mission when people started getting sick. Missions ceased.

In the corner, the lead actor had signed the poster with *Thank you for letting me be part of your dream.*

I smiled, excited to meet the person who the poster was signed for.

On the way out I saw a figure of the alien from *Home Away from Home,* holding up the books with its fifth arm. Another fabulous character brought to life by Elise Montgomery. The person who lived in this house had good taste. I practically bounded down the hallway in joy, opening the last door with excitement.

All that went away when I saw the woman lying there, the blue duvet pulled all the way up to her neck.

It took me a couple of seconds to recognize her, as the sickness had aged her skin, but once I knew, I couldn't contain my excitement. Everything clicked. The notes, the figures, the poster. I took a chair from the corner and pulled it up next to her.

"You're Elise Montgomery! Legendary sci-fi writer!" The chances of seeing her at all — of her surviving until now — were almost impossible. "Sorry," I whispered, realizing I'd shouted. "I'm Sarah. I'm a big fan."

She chuckled, then started coughing. When she moved to sit up, I instinctively put my hand out to help her, but she shooed me off.

"And you're a burglar, it seems. A nice one, though. Normally I would scream, but it's been so long since I've had any company."

"Me too." I wanted to explain more, but my mind went blank, too awestruck to correct her. She talked to me. To *me.*

Elise had given me hope that I could be whatever I wanted to be, and had shown me I could become an astronaut. She'd helped me fall in love with the stars, with exploring them. Where could I possibly begin that would make her understand?

"What's it like out there?" Elise asked. I blinked.

"It's . . . quiet," I finally settled on, though images of empty streets, broken houses, and still nights pushed to the front of my brain. In a way, it reminded me of space, of the vast silence there.

Elise gave a short nod and coughed again, deep and dry. Just like everyone else. My mom, my friends, my partner. Everyone that left me alone.

That was why I needed to make this museum. To remember I represented the world and humanity, still, even though so many had died.

"You can take anything you like. I won't need it anymore," she said, her voice hoarse.

I didn't get up, my confidence returning. "I'm not," I said.

"Hmm?"

"I'm not a burglar. You said I'm a burglar, but I'm not. I am — *was* — an astronaut."

She peered at me. "An astronaut?"

"Yes. I, well, I never got to go to space, but I . . ." I stared at my lap, suddenly feeling embarrassed.

"Me either."

I looked up. I always assumed Elise could describe the worlds outside ours so well because she'd participated in the astronaut program herself.

"Huh," was all I managed to say. Elise gave a small smile. I smiled back.

"So, it seems you've changed careers to survive. I understand. Take what you need."

"No. I, uh, I . . ." It felt strange to tell my hero about my life. What if she thought I was silly or immature? What if she agreed with my parents: going to space was a childhood wistful dream everyone had. I just happened to be stupid enough to follow it.

Elise kept her lips pursed, staring at me. She trusted the world with her words. Could I trust her with mine?

She'd given me so much. I could at least try.

"I'm creating a museum. I'm collecting things that represent humanity so that, uh, so that if aliens or something were ever to come here, they would know who we are, uh, were. That they would know that we fought to the very end, that we were more than our sicknesses."

She didn't respond for a moment, and I swore my heart stopped. But then she finally closed her eyes and sighed. "That sounds beautiful, Sarah."

I smiled, but Elise coughed again. I wanted to give her privacy, but my eyes darted to the tissue she held. It held blood, so I turned my gaze away, focusing on the window, on the way the light streamed in like tears.

"Can I get you anything? Water? Food?"

She shook her head. "I'm dying. Nothing will change that."

"I'm sorry."

"Don't be." She coughed again. "I lived a full life."

I resettled in the chair, my mind brimming with questions. What item did she want to contribute to the museum? What was her favorite movie or TV show she wrote? How did she get to where she was? What did she enjoy about writing, about the craft of putting pen to paper, then watching others make it reality? Did she think there really was life out there? What about *The Life of 234-O67*, the show that never got renewed? How would it end?

Elise inhaled and let her chest fall. I watched her, biting my tongue. By the time I felt ready to ask her everything, she'd fallen back asleep.

She rested quietly, not coughing at all. Content even. At peace.

I put my chair back into the corner, and went to leave the room, when I saw a small notebook with a pen on top, resting on her nightstand.

They would be the perfect things for my collection of humanity. The power of writing, of creation, of exploring a world beyond your own without ever leaving your room. The power of communication, of making dreams so powerful they influence reality.

"Thank you," I whispered as I grabbed the notebook and pen.

I couldn't watch her die, but I didn't want to leave her alone. In the end, I settled on something in between. Reaching into my pocket, I pulled out the one thing I kept from my time as an astronaut: my name badge. It still shined as though I'd received it yesterday, though the name had little scratches through it from sitting in my pocket these months. I put it on her chest as though it was a flower.

Then, with a deep breath, I went back downstairs, past the treasures of my childhood dreams, past the images and movies that had inspired me to explore, to never give up hope.

When I got to the door, I grabbed the burlap sack and left without a word. In a few more houses, my bag would be full and the Museum of Humanity would open.

ABOUT CAMDEN ROSE

Camden Rose is a queer author who loves seeking out magic beneath the everyday world. She can often be found at the ocean's edge taking notes on the local mermaid population. She lives in the Pacific Northwest with her spouse, black cats, and collection of books and board games. You can find her online at www.camdenscorner.com

The Last Star

Meghan E. Hart

I am waiting for the last star to go dark.

We all are.

The skies have been getting darker for a while now, each point in every constellation ceasing to sparkle, one at a time. The sun has continued rising and setting as it has done for as long as there have been people on this planet. The moon continues to move through its cycles, pulling and tugging at the tides.

All the other stars have been disappearing.

Every twinkle snuffing out. Dying, according to the scientists. The religionists have more dire explanations. But why it's happening doesn't really matter, does it? One by one, all the stars have gone dark, and now, other than our sun, there is only one left.

There's nothing we can do to stop it — the light we see from our last star was cast more than two million years ago. Whatever caused the stars to die happened long before we even existed. All we can do is wait. Watch. Wonder.

Scientists have predicted the moment of the final star's death. People all over the world are gathering to stare up at the sky, even if it's still too bright where they are for them to see the light go out. I'm lucky, I think, to be in a place where the skies are dark. I'll be able to make one last wish.

I'm waiting on the grassy hill where I used to take my children to see the Fourth of July fireworks. I'm waiting by myself, but I'm not alone. Some have brought picnic blankets, wine, charcuterie, desserts. I smell the tang of marijuana and wish for a small, spare moment that I'd thought to bring something to eat or drink, even though I'm not hungry and I don't want to be intoxicated for this. Nobody has been able to say for certain what the end of this last star will bring, if anything at all, but I want to be aware of whatever it is.

There are children here. Babies in arms, fussing and cooing. A toddler dances in front of her parents, begging for their attention. Her mother draws her into her lap and kisses the top of her curly head. Her shoulders shake as she cries, holding her daughter tight until the little girl squirms to be let free. Then she lets her go, because that is what we do with our babies. We might want to hold onto them forever, but eventually, we have to let them go so they can grow up.

Sometimes, we lose them.

Stars are born in nurseries, just like babies. They form in cauldrons of gas and dust, growing until they create new galaxies. There might be fresh baby stars out there somewhere, but they're so far away we cannot see their shine. Still, it gives me hope to think they are still being born. That one day, their blaze will reach the hopeful eyes of people looking up into blackness. My arms cradle emptiness, a memory of my own babies, long grown.

Long lost.

The lights from the city below us are dimming in preparation for what's to come. Some people protested the decision. Some people are ignoring tonight's event. Some people have even said it's no more than a hoax, despite the scientific evidence to the contrary.

The religionists have whipped some into a frenzy; those people are buried deep in bunkers and basements with their guns and supplies of freeze-dried food, confident that no matter what, they'll be saved because they believe.

Here on this grassy hill, my fellow sky-watchers are chatting and laughing. A short distance away in the shadows of some trees, I suspect a couple is making love beneath the cover of a large blanket, but what other people choose to do with their bodies is not my business, and I turn my gaze back to the sky.

The little girl dances over to me, keeping herself at a wary distance. "Hi."

"Hello," I say. She reminds me very much of my own daughter at that age, all bright eyes and tangled curls.

"Eliana, come back over here, please. Leave the lady alone," her mother calls.

Eliana frowns. "S'gettin' dark."

"Yes," I tell her. "But that's okay."

She tilts her small head. Puts small hands on her hips. "You have any kids?"

"I did. Yes."

And when they died, the light in my life went out. I was consumed by darkness. I tried to take comfort from looking up at the stars, imagining my children among them the way the religionists would have everyone believe.

It didn't work, and soon after, the stars started dying and that felt somehow more of a comfort, because if the stars didn't live forever, that meant nothing ever could.

"Eliana!"

Her mother stands, calls again, takes a step off the blanket.

Eliana looks over her shoulder. She braces to run with a grin on her face. This is a game to her, but I hear the rise of panic in her mother's voice. She's wishing she had not let her baby leave her arms, not now, not when we are so close to something none of us really understand.

The city goes dark.

The moon is a mere thin sliver of silver in the vast, black expanse of the universe, gazing down on us. All of us, so small. Insignificant in comparison to the rest of the universe but relentlessly important to ourselves.

People murmur. Laughter ceases. They embrace. Eyes turn upward.

There it is, the glimmer of the last star.

"One minute," someone says softly, and a countdown begins. It's like watching the ball drop in Times Square, but it quickly softens into silence before we get past thirty. This doesn't feel like a celebration.

We stand, heads tipped back. Swaying in unison. I am by myself, but not alone. We are all here together. We are all one.

The twinkle vanishes. We breath in. We breath out. We breath in . . . and hold it.

The final silver crescent of the moon disappears.

Our final star is gone.

The sky is inestimably blacker.

And we are rising up, up, into the sky above, into the darkness that is cold, but I am fiercely hot. I am on fire, burning. We're all burning. Twisting, flying, expanding. Making a brand-new galaxy.

We are all . . . stars.

As we leave our nursery, some of us have grown big enough to help make and sustain new worlds. Some align in shapes and patterns that will be given names by those who tell stories. Some of us only twinkle and dance and delight, but we are, all of us, stars. Our light casts itself out into the universe, traveling through space and time, and it finds new faces tipping upward to make wishes upon us.

I am by myself, but I am not alone.

I shine.

I shine.

Our WriteHive Anthologies

If you enjoyed *Rescuing Curiosity*, please consider also reading *Reclaiming Joy*, or any of the other WriteHive anthologies. Support our nonprofit by buying direct from our sponsoring partner Inked in Gray Press at InkedinGray.com. Proceeds from all WriteHive book sales are directly donated back to WriteHive!

www.ingramcontent.com/pod-product-compliance
Lightning Source LLC
Chambersburg PA
CBHW030855200726
48289CB00003B/767